Notes on a Near-Life Experience

Olivia Birdsall

Notes on a Near-Life Experience

Delacorte Press

Published by Delacorte Press
an imprint of Random House Children's Books
a division of Random House, Inc.
New York

www.randomhouse.com/teens

Educators and librarians, for a variety of teaching tools, visit us at
www.randomhouse.com/teachers

Library of Congress Cataloging-in-Publication Data
Birdsall, Olivia.
Notes on a near-life experience / by Olivia Birdsall.
p. cm.
Summary: Fifteen-year-old Mia feels like a ghost watching her own life when her parents' arguments escalate into a separation, triggering counseling sessions, strange behavior in her brother and sister, and a new connection with her brother's best friend.
ISBN: 978-0-385-73370-0 (trade edition)—ISBN: 978-0-385-90385-1 (glb)
[1. Family problems—Fiction. 2. Brothers and sisters—Fiction. 3. Divorce—Fiction. 4. Psychotherapy—Fiction. 5. Dating (Social customs)—Fiction. 6. California—Fiction.]
I. Title.
PZ7.B51198Not 2007
[Fic]—dc22
2006020439

The text of this book is set in 12-point Goudy.

Printed in the United States of America

10 9 8 7 6 5 4 3 2 1

First Edition

For Deb: my mom, soul mate, and centripetal force

Acknowledgments

Thanks to my editor, Stephanie Lane, and Delacorte Press for taking a chance on an unknown kid. I am indebted to my professors and classmates at Brigham Young University and New York University, especially Louise Plummer, Brian Morton, Breyten Breytenbach, Chuck Wachtel, and Nicole Hefner, for their input and encouragement. Mom, Dad, Erik, Anna, Lisz, Diana, David, Bekah, Michael, Zanna, and JohnEr, thank you for your love, inspiration, and patience.

Notes on a Near-Life Experience

prologue

GROWING UP, I WENT TO SCHOOL WITH THIS GIRL, JENNIFER Reebi, who had a mole about the size of a cherry pit in the middle of her left eyebrow. Her eyebrow, unaware of the existence of the mole, grew right over it, which made the mole that much worse, because not only was it big and conspicuous, it was hairy. Once in a while someone would show us how they could dislocate their finger at will, or they'd get an infected mosquito bite on their leg, an enormous zit on their forehead, or something equally gross that would take attention away from Jennifer's mole. But all those things were temporary, and the mole was permanent. No matter where she went, what she wore, who she sat with at lunch, Jennifer Reebi's mole was always there, obvious. You couldn't look at the girl and not focus on her mole, like how when you pass a really gruesome car accident, you slow down without even realizing it. Jennifer Reebi could have been brilliant, beautiful, the funniest, most interesting girl ever to live on earth, but in our minds she was a girl with a big, disgusting mole in the middle of her head. That mole ruled Jennifer Reebi's life; it defined her.

The fall of seventh grade, Jennifer Reebi returned to school moleless, with a normal eyebrow and everything. She had a teeny scar, but if you didn't know about the mole, you'd never suspect a thing. She was actually pretty cute. But she was still Jennifer Reebi, Mole Girl, and whenever anyone mentioned her or tried to describe her to someone else, they never failed to bring up the ugly mole she'd had over her eye. Her mole got bigger and hairier and uglier every time it was mentioned, and there was no immediate evidence to remind us of the truth. The legend of the mole was probably worse than the mole itself. Jennifer didn't even have a shot with new people; so many people remembered her mole that everyone else was bound to find out about it sooner or later. Her mole was inescapable. Back then, I couldn't imagine a fate worse than having Jennifer Reebi's mole, or even just having to live with its ghost. Then, miraculously, just before high school, Jennifer Reebi's family moved. If she's smart, I remember thinking, she'll forget about that mole and never mention it again.

If there's a moral to the story of Jennifer Reebi, a "main idea," as my English teacher always says—and I don't necessarily think there is one, but if there is—it's something about identity and society and escape.

But there's more than that.

Jennifer Reebi got to leave the ugliest thing in her life behind, while most of us are stuck on the side of the road as people slow down to catch a glimpse of our tragedies.

the way we were

When I was little, my parents held hands in public. Wandering through grocery stores, in movie theaters, at Linda Vista Elementary School's end-of-the-year carnival. Everywhere. It was embarrassing. They held hands even when we begged them not to. As a result of this constant hand-holding and all that went along with it, I am not an only child. There are three of us: my older brother, Allen, is seventeen, I'm fifteen, and my sister, Keatie, is eight. When I was in ninth grade, the hand-holding stopped, much to my relief. Maybe I wouldn't have been so relieved if I'd realized what that might mean.

Lately, my family has been different. My full-time family has always been my mom, Allen, me, and Keatie. My dad works a lot, so I think of him as more of a part-timer. He comes on vacations with us, is around on weekday mornings and Sundays, and occasionally stops in for dinner on weekdays. My mom complains a lot about how much he works, but the complaints haven't changed anything yet.

The full-time family has always been pretty tight, but lately things have been getting a little . . . loose. We used to hang out together; we'd sit at the same table and do homework while my mom paid bills, or we'd read magazines or play video games (okay, so I don't really play video games, but I'd be there when my brother and sister did). We even sat around and talked sometimes, like families on TV do. During the past few months, Mom has been working more, and Allen's been gone a lot. Keatie and I watch more TV and talk a lot less than we used to.

That doesn't sound like a big deal, probably, but it feels like a big deal to me. I mean, my family isn't boring, exactly, but we have routines:

—We eat dinner at seven o'clock every night, unless there's a dance performance or a violin recital or a soccer game or whatever going on. My dad only makes it to a couple of dinners a week—always on Sundays, and then usually at least one other day. He works a lot, even on weekends.

—Every Friday my brother and sister and I have pizza or Chinese food or some other kind of takeout for dinner, because that's my parents' "date night." When he's in a good mood, Allen gives them an obnoxious piece of advice like "Now, remember, Maggie"—that's my mom's name—"don't think that just because he buys you dinner you owe him something," and then he winks at her, or he'll remind my dad to use protection, or he'll tell them they have their whole lives ahead of them and they shouldn't put all that at risk for a few minutes of fun. He's big on making people as uncomfortable as humanly possible.

—On Saturdays we clean the house. Everyone, even my dad, has an assignment, and they can't do anything fun until they finish their assigned chore.

—My mom puts us each to bed every night. She doesn't tuck us in or anything, she just likes to talk to us before we go to bed. Most nights before I go to sleep, I tell my mom about school, and boys, and who said what about whom. I guess I tell her everything.

—My dad makes our lunches for school every night and puts them in the refrigerator for us so that they're ready and waiting for us in the morning. Unfortunately, he is a big fan of bologna sandwiches, and most of the rest of us aren't. My sandwiches usually end up in the garbage. Allen's friend Julian eats his every once in a while. I don't know what Keatie does with hers.

—Keatie, Allen, and I watch *Jeopardy!* together; sometimes Mom or Dad will watch with us. Okay, so we don't just watch it. We try to answer the questions, and sometimes we even keep score. (I never said these routines weren't embarrassing or ridiculous.) Or we'll each pick a contestant at the beginning and whoever's contestant wins doesn't have to do dishes.

—My dad takes one of us to lunch once a month. I think this was my mom's idea; when Dad started working a lot, we didn't see him much, and one night Keatie asked my mom when her real dad was coming home. My mom asked her what she meant by her "real dad" and Keatie said, "You know, the one who lives at home, like on TV. The dad we have lives at work." Mom sort of flipped out and Dad started picking us up from school every once in a while and taking us to lunch.

I didn't realize how much I depended on these habits, on the routine, on not having to think or worry about how my family functioned. I didn't realize how much I liked or needed our traditions. I think sometimes you have to lose things to see them for what they really are. Which sounds stupid and obvious and clichéd, like that song my mom sometimes listens to in the car about paving paradise and putting up a parking lot.

wheels of fortune

I GUESS I BEGAN TO NOTICE THAT SOMETHING WAS WRONG about three months ago. The three of us, Allen, Keatie, and I, were sitting in the living room, waiting for *Jeopardy!* to come on, watching *Wheel of Fortune* and guessing at the answer to a puzzle with only three letters—all *T*s—showing. It looked like this:

__ T __ __ __ __   __ __   T __ __   __ __ __ __ __ __ __ __
__ __ T __ __ __ __ __
Title

Keatie guessed, "*The Cat in the Hat* . . . no, wait . . . *Stand Up to* . . ."

I guessed, "*Stick My Toe* . . . *Italy Is Too* . . ."

Allen didn't bother guessing. "You guys suck. It's *Allen Rules the Universe, Obey His Every Command.*"

"Al, you always say that's what the answer is, and it never is," Keatie told him.

About then my parents came down the hall into the living room. They were arguing.

My dad said something like "I want you to stop acting like my mother, that's all."

And my mom said something like "I want you to stop acting like a child, then."

We didn't say anything.

I don't know what they were fighting about. It would have been easier to guess the answer to an impossible puzzle with three *T*s showing than to even begin trying to understand what was going on between them. And at that point, worrying about my parents' relationship seemed as unnecessary as finding the answer to a puzzle on a stupid TV show. They were fine, holding hands or not. There was nothing to see; we kept on driving, didn't even think about slowing down.

yorba linda

YORBA LINDA, CALIFORNIA, MY HOMETOWN, IS THE BIRTHplace of Richard Milhous Nixon, one of our nation's most misunderstood and underrated presidents, according to some Yorba Lindans. In the seventies no one really thought like that because he was the president and he hired burglars to spy on the Democrats or whatever, but I think people cut him a lot more slack now that he's dead. Yorba Linda is full of upper-middle-class people who have horse stables or swimming pools—sometimes both—in their backyards; people who think that because they own horses, they live in "the country" even though no one lives more than one point seven miles from a minimall; people whose patriotism moved them to change the name of our high school from West Hills to Nixon; people who get bored with their marriages after nineteen years.

In second grade, when my class toured the Nixon Library for a field trip, the tour guide told us that when the library had its grand opening, four U.S. presidents attended. At the time I believed that presidents were like kings and queens—that they had to die to leave office—so I didn't understand how four presidents could have attended at once. I'd always thought I lived in a magical place—after all, presidents are the closest things we have to royalty in America, and back then I expected everything in my life to be special, out of the ordinary. I lived where presidents came from. I had all these fantasies about my parents' sitting me down one day and telling me I was adopted and I was really Nixon's kid or grandkid, the offspring of a president, practically a princess. When I got home from the field trip, visibly disturbed, my parents found out what was wrong and tried to explain to me about elections. I almost threw a fit when they told me that presidents were only presidents for eight years at the most and that when they were done they went back home and found new jobs and lived nonpresidential lives like anyone else. Somehow grown-ups always managed to make things seem so ordinary; elections made Yorba Linda seem like any other place.

The realization that there was less magic in real life than I wanted there to be hit me hard, but after a while I built up some resistance. I try not to let those kinds of things get to me anymore. Usually, if you pretend you never believed to begin with, it doesn't feel like you've lost as much when you find out the truth.

sinkside seats to a battle of wills

LAST SATURDAY, DAD WAS AT WORK ALL DAY, AND IT WAS HIS job to clean the kitchen. So on Saturday night when he got home, my mom ripped him a new one.

"Russ, your job today was the kitchen, and it's still a mess." It's not like my mom to get upset about little things like this. But lately, she's been hypersensitive about my dad's not being home very much.

"Please, Maggie, I was at work all day, and now you want me to clean the kitchen? Give me a chance to rest. Have one of the kids do it. Tell Keatie I'll give her twenty bucks. She loves doing stuff to earn a little extra money."

"No way. This is your job. We care for this house together, remember? As a family."

"I'll clean the kitchen," I told them, "free of charge." It makes me uncomfortable when they get like this.

"That's okay, Mia. Your father will do his own work," my mom said.

"No, Maggie, I won't," Dad said. And he left the kitchen, walked out of the house, got in his car, and drove off.

I couldn't believe that my parents, two adults, were having such a ridiculous argument.

After Dad left, Mom said, "Mia, you will not clean a single dish or lift one finger to clean that kitchen, do you understand?"

"Why? This is so stu—"

"You heard me, young lady. This is your father's chore and he's going to do it."

I heard my dad come in late that night. I listened for voices, for some kind of an argument, but there was only silence.

Peace at last, I thought.

But the next morning the kitchen was still a mess, and my parents weren't speaking to each other. We all stayed out of their way, and out of the house, as long as possible. When I got home from my friend Haley's that night, just in time for dinner, the kitchen was clean, and we all ate together like we normally do on Sundays. I was too scared to ask what had happened. All that mattered was that things were back to normal.

family tree

IN FOURTH GRADE, MY CLASS DID THIS FAMILY HISTORY PROJECT where you had to fill out this chart and learn about who your grandparents were and stuff like that. When my teacher assigned the project, she said something about how we might be surprised who our ancestors were. Then she asked if any of us knew any stories about our relatives. A lot of my classmates raised their hands and talked about how they were related to famous people: Haley is related to Harriet Tubman, Steven Spielberg, and Shaquille O'Neal, somehow; Ana's ancestors came to America on the *Mayflower*; and Billy Lee's grandfather is the host of the most popular game show in Korea. I don't think I have a very interesting family history. My dad doesn't really tell me stories about his family. Instead, he talks a lot about Woody Allen. Woody Allen is this guy who makes movies that my dad really likes. I don't know much about my father's childhood or my ancestors, but I do know a lot about Woody Allen.

Most people my age don't really know who Woody Allen is. They are vaguely aware that he makes films and that he is *not* physically attractive. My mom says my dad wanted to be the next Woody Allen when he was in college, before Allen, Keatie, and I were born. My brother, sister, and I are named after Woody Allen and his leading ladies, as Dad calls them. My older brother's name isn't just Allen, it's Woody Allen Day, but if you ever called him Woody, he'd kill you. My full name is Mia Farrow Day, and Keatie is actually Diane Keaton Day. It's bizarre; I don't know why my mom agreed to it, but then again, when I think about the times when my parents fight about what octane of gas to put in the car, what movie to see, or who to vote for in the city elections, I wonder how and why they ever decided to marry.

From what I've seen of Woody Allen movies and from what I've heard on E! Entertainment Television, the man is a freak. He usually directs and stars in the films he writes, and he usually writes his character as a man who has lots of women falling all over him. Did I mention the fact that he looks like a computer programmer? He divorced Mia Farrow a while ago and married their adopted daughter or something. Very weird. If Mom ever had another baby girl—and she insists that she won't—her name would be Soon-Yi. That's the name of his third wife/daughter . . . Soon-Yi. I don't know what we'd do if she had a boy.

When I was younger, I'd go to my dad's office with him on Saturdays. I'd do homework, answer the few phone calls that came in, and go to the Korean market in his office complex to look at the octopus tanks and buy candy with flavors I'd never heard of, and when I got bored, I'd bug Dad until he took me to lunch. On our way to the office, he'd tell me stories about Mia Farrow, how beautiful she was, how she'd been married to an opera singer or musician or something before she met Woody. I'd listen and feel special to have been named after someone so famous and interesting, and I'd think that my dad knew everything about everything.

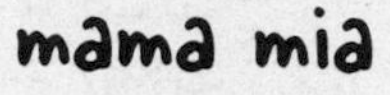

HE THOUGHT IT WAS A GREAT JOKE. MOST OF MY DAD'S JOKES are the kind that only he thinks are funny. He says the rest of us have no sense of humor.

When I was learning to talk, he'd point to my mom and then to me and say, "Mama . . . Mia . . . Mama . . . Mia." He's kept it up ever since—yelling for us to get in the car, looking for us at the grocery store, whenever the situation warrants.

"Mama, Mia . . . Mama, Mia."

He hasn't said it in months.

Last week, for instance, after my dance performance—which he nearly missed—when we were getting dessert, he was trying to get us all to hurry up and order, and he said, "Maggie, would you just make up your mind already?"

My mom just ignored him and kept looking at the menu.

So he turned to me and Keatie and said, "Girls, you know what you want, right?"

He usually says something like "Mama, Mia! What would you ladies like?" He usually gets a kick out of stuff like that, and Mom usually smiles at his jokes even if no one else does. Maybe we've all finally gotten tired of the old jokes.

I hope somebody comes up with some new ones soon.

paper or plastic?

ALLEN WORKS AS A BAGGER AT STATER BROTHERS, THE GROcery store near our house. Occasionally, he has to go out to the parking lot and round up the carts people leave scattered around because they are "too damn lazy to put their freaking carts in the damn cart corrals." I love it when Allen uses the words *cart corral.* I tease him about his bagger jargon-lingo-shoptalk whenever he gets going about cart corrals.

Anyway, when he first started working, my mom was really excited, and she went to the store and bought stuff just so Allen could bag it while she took his picture. I went along to watch.

"Mom, please. This is embarrassing," he said.

Mom ignored him and turned to the cashier. "I'm sure you see this all the time. Didn't your mother come visit you on your first day of your first job?"

The cashier, tired, mumbled something in support of my mother, who snapped another picture when Allen put the last bag into our cart.

"Nice apron," I said, gesturing to the worn crayon green uniform he wore. "Can I borrow it sometime?"

Allen ignored me. "Have a nice day. Thank you for shopping at Stater Brothers."

Sometimes I still go in, just to tease him.

My mom has been working a lot more lately. She used to do part-time consulting, but it's starting to feel like full-time. Anyway, the other day when I stopped in to say hi to Al at Stater Brothers, I was thinking about his first day, and I wondered if my mom will have time to come in and take pictures of me on my first day of work.

identity crisis

KEATIE WANTS TO PEE LIKE BOYS DO. SHE'S BEEN TRYING TO do it for years, ever since she was being potty trained and she found out that Dad and Allen got to pee standing up and aim at things. I'm willing to bet that Keatie has tried harder than any female in the history of the world to figure out a way for girls to pee standing up. She used to practice in our front yard until my mom realized what she was doing, and then she was relegated to the backyard, so as not to disturb the neighbors. Allen thinks it's great.

Her best friend, Chewy, who lives down the street, thought it was weird that she always asked him questions about how he peed. At that point, he might not have realized that she wasn't a boy, either.

Sometimes I wonder if Keatie should have been born a

boy, like those people on talk shows who say they're women trapped in men's bodies. She wears boys' underwear—maybe that goes along with the peeing thing, though. She's really into boxer shorts right now; before that, she liked briefs with superhero graphics on them. She doesn't have any friends who are girls because she thinks they're boring, and she's always trying to be like Allen—she plays soccer and video games like he does, likes the same foods he does. She even hangs around and hands him tools while he works on his car. They look a little bit alike, too: Keatie has this messy flaming red hair; Allen's is less red, more brown, but they look more related to each other than I do to either of them. I have straight brown hair.

Anyway, Keatie may just have an overactive imagination or an obsession with the identities of other people. Chewy has a Japanese exchange student named Toshi living with him. Since he came to stay, Keatie has been taping the sides of her eyes back to try to get them to look like Toshi's and using my mom's mascara to blacken her red hair. Which looks pretty hilarious, like she's in a neopunk band or something. Chewy's mom says that Keatie spends more time with Toshi than with Chewy these days, asking him questions he can't answer about Japan and Mount Fuji and samurai.

I don't blame her, really, for wanting to be somebody else.

the boy (almost) next door

I HAVE BEEN IN LOVE WITH JULIAN PAYNTER SINCE I WAS NINE. Every crush I have ever had has borne some resemblance, at least in my mind, to Julian. It's beyond pathetic. He moved in three houses down from us when I was in third grade and became Allen's best friend instantly—they're the same age, they both liked soccer, and they quickly decided that the only entertainment that came close to the exhilaration of the game was making fun of me. Sometimes I let them do it because I was willing to put up with just about anything to be in Julian's presence.

When I had braces and I had to wear headgear at night, I'd hide in my room whenever Julian came to sleep over so he wouldn't see me. When Allen figured out what I was doing, he and Julian busted into my room with aluminum foil on their teeth and coat-hanger contraptions wound around their heads, talking in lispy, spitty-mouthed voices and doing dance and cheerleading routines.

Julian's father left when Julian was seven—one of those guys who went to work one day and never came back, which doesn't usually happen around here. People in Yorba Linda get messy divorces or live in separate parts of the house and make each other miserable for years.

Now Julian's mom works a lot, so he spends a lot of time with our family. He even comes on family vacations with us. Sometimes my romantic fantasies were challenged by things like my mother's talking in front of Julian about how I needed to wear a training bra, or Julian and Allen's telling me to leave them alone so they could pick up girls at the hotel pool. Still, I hold on to the dream.

The three of us, Julian, Allen, and I, are almost friends now. The teasing has stopped, at least, and occasionally, they'll let me catch a ride with them to a school activity or a concert or something, but Allen never fails to tell me that the only reason I am allowed to tag along is because of his goodwill toward me. He loves to remind me how Julian's mom, Hope, used to make them invite me to go to the movies with them when we were younger so I wouldn't feel left out. Back then, I'd try to pretend Julian was my date, but that became difficult when he and Allen would make me sit at least three rows away from them, a practice that continues, though unspoken, to this day.

I gave up the dream of Julian being my first kiss in sixth

grade when I had to kiss Billy Chin during a game of Spin the Bottle at Julie Scudelari's thirteenth birthday party, but I still harbor the insane hope that one day Julian Paynter will fall madly in love with me. Sometimes when Allen's at work or busy, Julian and I will end up hanging out together because he doesn't like being home alone, and I find myself pretending he's my boyfriend.

I don't think he notices.

playing games

↕

TODAY JULIAN IS AT OUR HOUSE PLAYING VIDEO GAMES WHILE Allen is at work. I am pretending to do homework while secretly watching him.

He shouts at me from the game he is playing, "I still haven't died. Can you believe I've gotten this far on one man?"

"I can*not* believe that," I say, trying to sound genuine. I hate video games; they seem so pointless.

My goal is to do two math problems every five minutes. If I do them fast enough, I can stare at Julian for two or three of those five minutes and still get my homework done before Al gets home.

"Aaaaaahhhhh, nooooo!" Julian yells. "So close, so close." He turns off the game and turns to look at me. "I let you down, Meezer. I was going to win that game for you, and I died. Will you ever look at me the same again?"

"Never," I tell him. He's never tried to win for me before. Does that mean something? I'll have to ask someone who knows about the symbolism of video games in the male psyche.

"Cool. How will you look at me, then?"

"I will see a three-toed sloth every time I look at you." Why do I say these things?

Julian looks confused, or maybe embarrassed. "Do you want to go and take all the carts out of the cart corral at Staters and see what Al does?" he asks.

"Nah, I've got homework," I say without thinking.

"Oh." He almost looks disappointed.

And before I can take it back, before I can straighten out my brain and say "*Yes!* I will go anywhere you want me to go!" Julian is putting his backpack on and heading for the stairs.

Sometimes I get confused about where the dividing line is between the world I actually live in and the dream dimension where Julian could see me as something other than his best friend's annoying little sister.

weekend getaway

↕

THE FIRST TIME I EVER SAW MY MOTHER CRY, OUTSIDE OF A movie or an art exhibit—you know, cry about something of her own—was when I was eleven. She had planned a surprise weekend trip for the two of them, her and my dad. They were just going to San Diego, which is only like an hour away, but she'd gotten my aunt Laura to come over and babysit, and she'd promised to bring us back presents if we behaved ourselves. She had this little suitcase all packed. Dad had said he'd be home by seven. Seven came and went; then eight, then nine. Mom sat on the couch, waiting. She called Dad several times, but he didn't answer his phone.

"He must be caught in traffic," she kept saying, more to herself than to us. "He may have had a last-minute meeting . . ."

At nine-thirty she put us to bed. While she was saying

good night to me, she stopped suddenly, was quiet for a moment. In the dim light of my room I watched as she tried to catch her breath and covered her mouth to stop any sounds from escaping. I saw her wet, crumpled face and I felt helpless. I couldn't say anything. I pretended that I hadn't noticed anything, which made me feel worse, but I didn't know what else to do.

My dad came home later that night, and when we woke up in the morning, they were gone. On Sunday night they came home with presents for each of us, as promised, and my mom's face glowed, no trace of hurt or sadness in it.

There's something about that moment in my bedroom, though—her face, seeing things I wasn't meant to see—that haunts me. I can't think about it without feeling scared and old.

dam breaks

My parents have been arguing a lot, but they've tried to hide it from us. Most nights after Dad comes home, Mom follows him back to their bedroom. I guess they think that shutting the door provides some kind of soundproof barrier, that it isolates them and their fight. It's true, we don't hear much of what they say—not many words, at least—but it's difficult to miss the general feeling of anger and hostility that emanates from the room along with the muffled sounds.

When they begin to yell, when *Mom* begins to yell, we catch little snippets of what they are saying.

"Why can't you just . . ."

"Did you ever stop to think that . . ."

"I'm doing the best I can here!"

"You never . . ."

"We never . . ."

"I don't . . ."

Mom's yelling usually starts Dad yelling, too, but they always catch themselves and lower their voices before they finish a sentence. Mom usually leaves the house to "run some errands" after these "discussions." We act like everything is fine, but we know something is going on. Dad has started leaving for work early in the morning and rarely comes home before we are asleep. He shows up for dinner once in a while, but he camps out in his study with the door shut as soon as dinner is over. Mom seems to be working more, too; at least, she's been home less and less.

Like I said, they keep us out of whatever's going on, so when Mom brings up an unfinished argument during dinner tonight, I am surprised.

"So what's your excuse this time? Some big deal that you had to finish up? Cocktails with a client that you couldn't miss?"

Dad isn't too excited about having his meal interrupted. "Maggie, I don't want to discuss this here . . . now. . . . Can we please just eat in peace?" He shoves a forkful of salad into his mouth for emphasis. Some of the lettuce doesn't make it all the way in.

"You don't want to discuss it anywhere; that's the problem. You don't want to discuss it with a counselor—at least, you don't show up for most of our appointments. You don't want to discuss it with me here in the house, so you stay away from home. Tell me where you would like to discuss it. I don't think the place exists." Mom puts her fork down and pushes her chair away from the table.

Counseling? Missed appointments? What are they talking about? Or not talking about? What are they *supposed* to be talking about? And why haven't they talked to us about it? I look at Allen for some sign of what we should do—stay at the table, leave, ask questions, keep our mouths shut.

"Mom, how long do I have to wear my braces? They aren't doing anything. My teeth look exactly the same as they did before," Keatie whines, baring her teeth for emphasis.

If Allen or I made a comment like that, it would probably be an attempt to change the subject or steer my parents away from an argument and toward a less volatile line of conversation. However, I don't think Keatie has any such motive. She refuses to believe that there is ever anything very wrong with the world. She sees those commercials on TV about starving kids and honestly believes that somehow they got that skinny between lunch and dinner. When my parents fight, it worries me; Keatie thinks it's normal, that they're not really fighting at all. And the question about when she's going to get her braces off? She's had them for three weeks.

"Keat, they've told you a million times that it'll take at least another year," Allen snaps. He knows all about Keatie's orthodontia because he takes her to most of her appointments. My mom started working again shortly after Al got his driver's license; he got his car in exchange for agreeing to drive Keatie and me around. When I get my driver's license, I, too, will have the privilege of driving Keatie to the orthodontist, violin lessons, and soccer games.

Mom ignores the orthodontic conversation and addresses Dad. "I'm asking you if you are willing to work . . . and compromise . . . make some changes . . . do something for this family. Do you care at all about what's going on here?"

There is a pause, too long and very awkward, between Mom's question and Dad's reply. In the four seconds it takes Dad to come up with his answer, we've heard something else. He *doesn't* know, not for sure; maybe he *doesn't* care. I'm not sure what he and Mom are talking about, exactly, but it feels like we're all involved in it somehow.

"Of course I care. What kind of a question is that?"

But it's too late. Dad's answer doesn't feel like the right one, the one Mom wants, maybe the one *we*'d want if we knew what her question meant. It feels like an answer we shouldn't have heard. My chest tightens. I feel like I'm suffocating. My face feels like it's on fire. It's strange how sometimes you can understand an answer without even knowing the question, kinda like on *Jeopardy!* Dad's answer tells me that something is broken in my family and that it's probably something I can't fix, especially since I don't really know what has fallen apart.

I get up from the table as quietly as I can and mumble something about great dinner and homework to do; Allen does the same, dragging Keatie along with him, leaving Mom and Dad alone at the table.

I go to the bathroom and stare at myself in the mirror, looking for a change in the way I look, any indication that I'm defective, that I'm part of a defective family. It's difficult to focus, though, and I wish I could just close my eyes, make myself disappear. I feel weak and tired. A wave of nausea hits me. The toilet is too far away, so I aim for the sink and I throw up—spaghetti and Caesar salad from the dinner I've just eaten. The dinner where Dad's pause made us wonder whether he loved us enough to "compromise" or "make some changes." The dinner where Keatie complained that her braces weren't moving her teeth fast enough. The dinner where my life began to parallel a bad soap opera. I drink water straight from the faucet, trying to rid myself of the sour, acidic taste in my mouth.

After a few minutes of puking and rinsing, I feel clean. Like everything bad has been emptied out of me. I focus on this feeling. I want to hold on to the sense that what's happened is over. Gone. A temporary bad taste.

I spend the rest of the night in my room, staring at my math homework, then my English homework, then my social studies homework, then the math again, my cell phone turned off, my stereo turned up.

After a few hours, Allen knocks on my door. "Are you okay?"

"Sure."

"I just wanted to check and see."

He stands in the doorway, waiting for me to say something. I don't.

"I think maybe they're going to get a divorce. They've been fighting a lot lately," he says.

I don't say anything. For some reason, I'm mad at Allen for suggesting that they might be splitting up; it feels like he's giving up, making it happen by saying it.

"Well, good night," he says.

"Night."

coming of age

↕

I WANT TO KNOW HOW ADULTS DECIDE WHEN THE TRUTH IS necessary and when it isn't, and if there's some kind of an age requirement for it. Like, does getting a driver's license or the right to vote also mean it's time for you to know why your aunt Lucinda was in that hospital for two months when you were eight, or what really happened to your dog when it mysteriously vanished three weeks after its fourteenth birthday?

The strange thing is that the truth has this way of seeping through, leaking out, even when you build walls and dams and work as hard as you can to contain it. It's like even when no one tells you what the truth is, somehow, eventually, you just feel it. Even if you don't want to.

three days later

SATURDAY MORNING. JULIAN, ALLEN, AND KEATIE ARE UP-stairs playing video games; I'm in the basement working on the piece I'm choreographing for a competition. I go up to my room to find some different music and Dad emerges from his and Mom's room with a suitcase.

"Allen," he calls, "come here and help me."

I grab a mix CD from my room and pause at the staircase to see what's going on.

Al comes down the hall with Keatie following.

"I want to help, too," she says.

"I don't think I have anything small enough for you to take," Dad tells her.

"What are you doing?" Al asks Dad, eyeing his suitcase.

"I need your help getting my things into my car," Dad says.

"Why?"

"Allen, please. Take this out to the car."

Allen doesn't say anything; he turns and goes back down the hall, leaving Dad with the suitcase.

Dad drags the suitcase down the hall. Keatie and I watch without saying a word. We go to the balcony and look on as Dad struggles to load it into his trunk.

I feel like I'm dreaming, like this can't be happening, because you're supposed to be able to feel things like this coming, but I didn't. Or maybe I wouldn't, or just didn't want to? I wonder if this is how all families come apart—so quietly and unexpectedly that you are numb by the time the biggest blow hits. I decide it's probably better not to feel anything at all than to feel everything at once and break under the weight. Like this girl Tracy at my school: her parents split up and she stopped wearing makeup and doing her homework; she fell apart.

Allen wanders out to the driveway, watches Dad pack up, pretends to practice footwork with his soccer ball. Julian comes out, helping Dad carry the remainder of his suitcases and boxes from the house to his car. When they've finished, Dad thanks Julian and shakes his hand.

Keatie rushes out to the driveway, hugs Dad, and asks, "Where are you going?"

"I'm going to be staying in a condo across town. Your mother asked me to leave."

"Why?" Keatie asks.

Dad hugs her again, then gets in his car and drives away. I

realize at this moment that my father has never explained anything to me; it's always been my mom: Santa, sex, quadratic equations, it was always Mom. I wonder what I will miss about my father, if I will miss him at all, and I am scared.

Julian and Keatie are the only ones who seem choked up when he leaves. Mom doesn't come out of her room until that evening, when she asks Allen to go pick up some Chinese food for dinner. I feel stronger, smarter than her for not being paralyzed the way she is. For the first time in my life, she offers no explanations. Maybe because we haven't asked the right questions, any questions. Maybe because this is too big for an explanation. Maybe she doesn't know how to explain. Maybe there is no explanation.

what i want to be when i grow up

↕

LAST SUMMER WHILE OUR FAMILY WAS ON VACATION IN Mexico, I met this guy named Miguel. He had an accent that made him seem more attractive than he really was—I can see that now when I look at the pictures. Anyway, he really wanted to be a veterinarian. He talked about it a lot: how he "loffed aneemahls," how "ees barry hard go to betreenahrian school." I couldn't figure out why anyone would want to spend their life neutering cats. I mean, *really* want it.

My mom used to paint and sculpt; she studied art in college. She works in public relations now. She plans art openings once in a while—I think that's the closest she comes to actually making art. Allen, Keatie, and I bought her a potter's wheel last Christmas and she got pretty emotional when she opened it, but she's never used it. I found it in the garage last week when I was looking for a box of my old dance costumes. A heavy, dusty box with a picture of a smiling, muddy, fully clothed couple on the front, clay on a wheel in front of them—a G-rated version of the sexy pot-throwing scene from that movie *Ghost*. I imagined my mom and dad making pots together. I pictured them arguing and throwing mud in each other's faces rather than smiling happily.

My dad spent nine years earning his PhD in film studies, and now he sells commercial real estate.

When I say that I want to be a dancer—"the next Martha Graham," my mom says—and they tell me that I can do it, that I can be anything I want—I'm not sure I believe them.

does the absence of bologna make the heart grow fonder?

THE MONDAY AFTER DAD LEFT, I WAS EATING A BOWL OF cereal in the kitchen and Keatie came in. She opened the door of the refrigerator, stared inside it for a few seconds, and then closed it.

"Mo-om," she yelled. "Nobody made lunches."

Mom came in half dressed, her hair still wet. "What's going on, sweetie?"

"There's no lunch in here. Dad usually makes me a lunch."

"Oh, that's right, I forgot. Well, I'll give you some money for a school lunch today, and then we'll decide what to do for the rest of the week tonight, okay?"

Keatie frowns. “But I don’t like the lunches they make at school. I want bologna.”

My mom sighs. “Keatie, it’s just one day, then we’ll figure something out.”

“It isn’t just one day. Dad made the sandwiches and now he’s not here. Tell him to come back. Tell him it’s for the bologna.”

I rinse my bowl in the sink and tune out the rest of their conversation, wondering how it is that the lack of a bologna sandwich may be the thing we notice most about my father’s absence.

like two peas . . .

I MET MY BEST FRIEND, HALEY, ON THE SECOND DAY OF FIRST grade. Actually, it was my first day of first grade, her second. I was supposed to be in kindergarten that year, but when I got to class on the first day, the teacher found out that I already knew how to read, tie my shoes, and add.

"Do you know your address?" she asked.

"Two nine oh one El Rancho Via, Yorba Linda, California. Nine two eight eight six," I said.

She left me in the chair where she'd been interrogating me since she'd found me reading *Make Way for Ducklings* and spoke in loud whispers to the other teacher.

"What am I supposed to do with her?" She acted as if I'd done something horribly wrong.

They decided to call my mother. The next thing I knew,

I'd been kicked out of kindergarten and put in first grade. I wasn't a child genius. I knew how to read because Allen did. I'd had no idea I was transforming myself into some kind of freak by learning to read, tie my shoes, add, and recite my address.

So I met Haley on the second day of first grade. I thought she must have been a princess or a giant, she was so tall—taller than all the kids in first and even second grade. I was pretty short, I guess, so that made her seem even taller. When the teacher had us draw pictures of ourselves, Haley's looked different than everyone else's: she had a neck in her picture, and her arms weren't drawn as short as the rest of ours.

Our teacher, Ms. Beccia, assigned me the desk next to Haley's, and it just made sense for us to be friends since we had to share paste and stuff.

We've had disagreements: I used to want to hold her hand all the time—it felt natural since she seemed almost as tall as my mom—and she didn't like it; she wanted us to take tennis lessons together, but I was more interested in dance; she wanted us to dress up as cowgirls one Halloween, but I wanted us to be princesses. At some point it must've dawned on us that we didn't have to be clones to be friends.

Now I make up dances and Haley practices tennis. I dream about kissing Julian Paynter and Haley dreams about finding a guy who is taller than she is but who doesn't think basketball is the only reason to live. I hang up flyers for the spring dance concert and Haley writes the phone number for the Rwandan

Relief Fund on the chalkboard of every classroom in school. Between the two of us, we can talk about anything.

But I feel that saying something out loud makes it more true. Final. I haven't told Haley about my parents. It feels like telling her will make this whole mess real. Right now, there are some things I'm not ready to finalize.

headshrinking—session 1

↕

My dad decided that Allen, Keatie, and I needed therapy if we were ever going to be normal again once he moved out. I think it's the Woody Allen thing; all the people in Woody Allen movies see analysts, but they're all weirdos who live in New York City and have affairs with their sister's husband or their girlfriend's best friend. Mom agreed to take us to a shrink, but only if she got to pick him. These are the things they argue about. Like they are children. Mom's friend Eileen recommended Dr. Lynder. I had no say in the matter.

So here I am, sitting on the leather couch in the waiting room, reading *People* magazine, trying to guess what Dr. Lynder will be like.

I wonder if he'll try to seduce me. That's what always happens in the movies. You know, a young, innocent girl, a bit unstable, goes to a shrink, and the next thing you know she's thinking, He's the only one who really understands me. One thing leads to another. . . . You get the picture. Ba-da-boom, ba-da-bing. . . . And then when the girl tries to expose the psychiatrist after she figures out that what's going on isn't right, after she regains some of her sanity, he diagnoses her as delusional and has her locked up, along with his other victims.

The receptionist tells me to fill out a paper with a bunch of statements on it that you have to rate from one to five, one being never and five being always. They are questions like:

My life is of value.

I am loved by others.

I love myself.

I contemplate suicide.

Questions for crazy people. Any reasonably intelligent person can figure out what the right answers are. It's pretty easy. I put in some twos and fours on the less crazy questions so that it will look like I've really thought hard about the questions and my true feelings.

The door to Dr. Lynder's office opens and a man and a woman step out. The woman looks like she's about twenty-five; she has long ice blue fingernails and wears leather pants. The man is balding and fairly nondescript. I imagine myself falling asleep during our sessions.

"See you next week," the woman calls after the man as he heads for the door. The man grumbles as he leaves. Before I can stop him, before I realize what's happening, my boring, balding therapist is out the door, leaving me with the blue-clawed bimbo. She notices me before the door closes behind the man. "You must be Mia," she says, smiling down at me. "I'm Lisz Lynder."

"Yeah, umm, hi." I don't know what to say. I mean, I don't know why I assumed my doctor would be a man. When I get a closer look at Lisz Lynder, I notice some little lines around her eyes and mouth; I realize that she probably isn't as young as I thought, probably closer to my mom's age than to twenty-five.

"Whaddya say we go back to my office and talk a little," Lisz Lynder suggests.

I follow her through the door she and the bald man just came out of.

During my first visit, Lisz—she says I should call her by her first name, "Dr. Lynder's too formal"—explains that we'll talk about whatever I want to talk about and that nothing I say will ever leave this room unless I give my express permission or if she suspects that I have plans to harm myself. I must not look very thrilled about what she's said.

"Mia, why don't you tell me why you are here and what you hope to gain through your visits."

"To tell you the truth, I didn't want to come here. My parents thought that all us kids should get counseling because of, you know, the separation. So my brother, Allen, and I are going to visit you, and my sister, Keatie, is seeing someone who specializes in helping younger kids. I think the whole thing is ridiculous. I mean, my parents are the ones who need counseling, not us."

Lisz isn't fazed by my answer. She says that if I don't feel like I have anything to say, that's fine. She also says that if it's okay with me, she'll think up some topics for us to talk about, write them on pieces of paper, and put them in a jar. Then if I feel like I need help figuring out what to "discuss," I can take a piece of paper out of the jar and talk about what it says. If I don't like one topic, I can choose another paper and another until I find something I am willing to discuss. Or we don't have to talk about anything.

"If worst comes to worst, if you don't feel like chatting, we'll play Uno or something," she says.

I try to smile.

"But I want you to understand what I hope to do here as well. I am not going to tell you what's wrong with you, or tell you what you need to do to be a happy person or anything like that. My approach to therapy is a little different. I believe that we all possess the faculties we need to be happy; we just need to learn how to access them. So we're going to talk and you're going to find your own answers, a way to live that works for you. I'm going to be your guide, in a way. . . . If you ever get lost or really off track, I'll help you find your way back, and I'll try to help you understand what's going on in your life and what your options are for coping with certain situations. Everyone sees the world differently and has a different set of values, so we're going to figure out what yours are and help you be true to them. How does that sound?"

"Great," I manage to respond. What am I supposed to say? "It sounds like a load of crap and I can't believe you get paid for this?" "Excuse me, I can talk to myself for free?" "Did you graduate from an accredited institution of higher learning or earn your degree through a correspondence course?"

So now I have my own shrink, my own Dr. Marlena Evans from *Days of our Lives*. But the whole thing seems weird: talking to a stranger about the things that are most personal and important to you; paying someone to listen to you. Why would they care? They don't even know you; you could tell them whatever you wanted and they'd never know if it was true. Besides, I don't even know what's really going on. I don't like the idea of someone else figuring my family out, figuring my life out, before I do. And what if she gets it wrong? What if she sees things I don't, or things I don't want to see?

my brother, the boy scout

Today on the way to school a dog runs out into the road, and Al swerves and slams on his brakes to avoid hitting it. Al's backpack is open and its contents spill onto the floor of the van. As I'm shoving his stuff back in, I notice a small silver canteenish thing among the pencils and notebooks.

"What's this?" I ask him, shaking the silver container. I can hear liquid swishing around in it. "A canteen?"

Allen looks nervous. "Yeah. You know, instead of carrying one of those stupid plastic water bottles, I use that. . . . It looks cooler."

"Yeah, I guess, but it doesn't hold much. You know what it looks like? A flask, like some bum on the street or a secret agent would carry. I've never seen one before, but this totally looks like it could be one."

He laughs. "A flask? Yeah, the principal would love it if I brought a flask to school, huh?"

He's weird sometimes, my brother.

untouchables

HALEY OBSERVES THE SOCIAL SYSTEM AT OUR HIGH SCHOOL like she's doing a study for *National Geographic*. "Even the bathrooms are divided up, Meems. Do you know that we've always naturally used the bathrooms for popular kids, even though no one ever told us to?"

"What are you talking about?" I've never really considered myself a popular person. I wear normal clothes, go to normal parties, have normal friends. I guess I've just assumed that my life is normal, that I'm normal. Maybe things are really better, or worse, than I thought. Maybe I'm popular, or maybe I'm an outcast who hasn't been using the right bathroom.

"Have you ever used the bathrooms in the math building or the ones near the industrial technology building?"

"Math building, no. And I have no idea what industrial technology is."

"Exactly. We're naturally stratified. We're practically living in a caste system, you know, like in India, where there's a whole class of people whose existence no one will acknowledge. There are some really freaky kids in those bathrooms, too."

Haley has a flair for the dramatic. But I wonder about the bathrooms. And the people and things I've never bothered to notice.

kiki-short-for-kirsten

↕

KIKI NORDGREN IS PERFECT. HER FAMILY IS RICH, SHE HAS A perfect body, and she has the third-highest GPA in the senior class. The only imperfect thing about Kiki is the fact that she is perpetually pissed off. Of course, I could be biased because she has never really liked me. And things only got worse when I was chosen to be a dance team choreographer and she wasn't; she's a senior and I'm just a junior. So I should have known something was up last July during dance clinics, when Kiki kept wanting to come over and practice with me, when she was nice to me for no reason, and when she kept offering to pick me up in the mornings.

"Well, you *are* one of the only girls on the team who doesn't drive, so I thought I'd ask." Big smile.

I noticed that she kept finding reasons to wander around

the house in her skimpy dance clothes, but I was too dumb to figure out why until the day I found Kiki in the driveway talking to Allen and Julian while they were rebuilding the engine of Allen's 1973 VW bus. She'd gone upstairs to get some water and had been gone for twenty minutes.

"Is your name really *Kiki?*" Allen was asking.

"Kiki's short for Kirsten," she said.

"It sounds kind of like . . . ummm . . . ," Julian started to say.

"Norwegian?" Kiki said.

"No, not that," Julian said, "like a trained seal or something, you know?"

I laughed out loud. Kiki looked at me like she was going to eat me alive.

Allen piped up, "No, dude, I think it sounds Norwegian. I really do."

And that's where it all began. I think Kiki would have been happy to date either Allen or Julian, but since Allen was the guy who stepped up and defended her heritage, Kiki chose him. When Allen dumped Kiki the day before the dance team fund-raising car wash six weeks later—"She's just too intense. . . . Man, she's intense," he told me—she called Julian a few times, but he ignored her, thank goodness. The only thing that could possibly be worse than Kiki's dating your brother would be Kiki's dating the boy you're in love with. She went back to despising me, only with much greater intensity: she hasn't come to pick me up for practice since then, but she *has* made a point of suggesting major changes to most of the pieces I choreograph and talking about her endless stream of dates very loudly in front of me whenever she gets a chance. She told everyone on the dance team that she was sure I had something to do with Allen's dumping her. If I had, I would have most definitely taken credit for it. Unfortunately, my brother has never been one to take the advice of others, however wise or sensible it may be.

the sandwoman

TONIGHT WHEN I GET INTO BED AND TRY TO FALL ASLEEP, something seems off. It takes me a while to figure out what it is: no Mom. She hasn't come in to talk to me about my day and say good night. I lie there and wait for her to come in. And I wait. And I wait. But there's nothing. She doesn't come.

I get out of bed and walk down the hall to the bathroom near the living room, under the pretense of getting a glass of water, to see if she's awake and watching TV or something. Maybe she got really tired and fell asleep while she was watching it. But I don't hear any noise, so I go out into the living room and investigate. The clock on the DVD player says 11:23. Mom is nowhere to be found. The house is quiet.

I start back toward my room and run into Keatie in the hall.

“What are you doing up so late?” I ask.

“Looking for Mom. She never came.”

“She’s not out there,” I tell her. “Go back to bed.”

“No,” she says. “I’m getting Allen. He’ll do it.”

She knocks on his door, and I go back to my room. So Mom misses a night; do I really need someone to tuck me in every night? I know I shouldn’t, but I feel like I do. I go over all the things I would have told Mom in my head, but it isn’t the same.

drive

BECAUSE I SKIPPED KINDERGARTEN, I'M PRACTICALLY THE only person in the entire junior class who can't drive; I won't be sixteen until May. As far as I know, the only other person who can't, besides the kids in those remedial classes, is Barrett Waterson, this guy who got so many speeding tickets that his license was revoked about a month after he got it. I'm supposed to take my driving test the day after my birthday, because my birthday is on Sunday this year.

Until I get my license, I'm only supposed to drive with my parents, and no one else is allowed to be in the car with us when I drive. It's California law. Apparently, Allen is above this law.

"Nobody obeys that rule. You need an enema," Al tells me. "Listen, if you fail your driving test, I'm not going to drive you anywhere anymore. And I am sick of being the only one who can drive Keatie around."

"But if I get caught, they won't let me get my license."

"It's like two point eight miles from the school to our house. You won't get caught. And even if you do, just act like you didn't know the rule and they'll give you a warning. C'mon, get in."

He hands me the keys and walks over to the passenger side of the VW bus. I fumble with the keys and open the door on the second try. I get in and reach across the car to open Allen's door. He hops in and immediately puts on his seat belt.

He's been doing stuff like this a lot lately, acting like now that my dad is gone, he needs to do the things Dad would do: teach me to drive, tell me to go to bed, make sure I'm not hanging out with anyone sketchy.

"Let's just take it easy, okay, Meems? No fancy stuff."

"If you're so nervous, why are you making me drive?"

"I'm doing this for your own good, little sis. I'm older than you. And wiser. And I know that even if it means I have to put my life on the line, you have to learn to drive and begin your journey into womanhood."

"Shut up."

"Okay, I'm going to have to ask you to take some deep breaths and count to ten. I can't let you drive angry. It isn't safe."

"This coming from the king of road rage? The boy who followed an eighty-year-old woman for twelve miles because she cut him off? Give me a break."

He ignores my comment. "Now that you've relaxed a little, you may start the car and back out slowly, checking your mirrors and looking over your shoulder to make sure that no one is behind you," he says in a slow, nasal voice.

"I know all that already. I swear if you don't stop acting like a driving instructor, I am going to drive this thing into the nearest light post. Stop talking and let me concentrate."

"Okay, okay."

I begin to back out and immediately a horn sounds. I look over my shoulder. Kiki Nordgren and her best friend, Gabi Huang, are right behind us in Gabi's car, waving their hands in the air and giving us dirty looks.

"Well, at least you almost hit someone worth hitting. Good form," Allen says. "Now use your mirrors and check over your shoulder this time, and pull out slowly."

I turn the car off, take the keys out of the ignition, look at them, turn to Al, and say, "Keys can be dangerous weapons, you know."

"No more driving instructor, I promise."

I start the car again, check the mirrors, look over my shoulder, and pull out slowly.

living dead girl

↕

I'VE STARTED TO FEEL LIKE A GHOST. LIKE I'M ALIVE AND DEAD at the same time. Like I can see things but people can't see me as much. Like things happen but I don't feel them the same way I used to.

I'm not as excited these days when good things happen—we were invited to a regional dance competition that only twelve teams in the state get to attend, but it doesn't feel like a big deal.

I'm not as disappointed when bad things happen—I forgot that I had a midterm in my science class, I didn't study for it, and I got the second-lowest grade in the class.

Once, on *Oprah*, she had this panel of guests who had all died and then come back to life, like they were resuscitated after they hadn't breathed for a couple of minutes, stuff like that. They called what had happened to them "near-death experiences." And they talked about how amazing it was to know what death was like and still be able to live. I feel like I'm having a near-life experience, like I used to be alive and I know what that's like but now I'm doing something else. I don't want to die or anything. I just feel like I'm not as alive as I used to be.

another visit to the headshrinker

↕

I SAW THIS TALK SHOW ONCE WHERE ONE OF THE GUESTS WAS this man who was such a compulsive liar that he'd lost the ability to distinguish between the lies he told and reality. His wife said that to save their marriage he needed to get help. His psychiatrist made him start making lists of what he knew was true and what wasn't, and he had to learn what the truth was and how to tell it all over again. The guy said that sometimes he still lied for no reason, just out of habit; that sometimes he'd tell his wife a story and then immediately he'd have to tell her he was lying. I sit in Lisz's office and wonder what would happen if I lied to her. Would I forget what was real and what wasn't? Do I really even know the truth anyway?

"Anything you want to talk about today, Mia?" Lisz asks.

I stare. "I want to talk about condiments and their classification in the food pyramid."

"Well, I don't know a lot about that topic, but if you'd like to discuss it, I'd be more than happy to listen," she says.

It's not easy to be contrary when someone is so willing to agree with you. I don't think I have fifty minutes' worth of condiment talk in me.

Lisz has made a jar full of topics to discuss, like she said she would. She's taped a neon pink piece of paper to it that says, LET'S TALK ABOUT . . . , and filled it with different-colored slips of paper that I assume all have "interesting topics" written on them. It sits conspicuously in the middle of the coffee table that separates her chair from the couch I sit on.

I grab the jar and take out a bright orange slip of paper: *your first experience with divorce*. How convenient, I think. I wonder if every single slip of paper in that jar says the same thing, or some variation of it, so that we can talk about whatever Lisz wants to. Maybe she'll change the papers every week depending on what she wants to talk about.

"Okay. It says, 'your first experience with divorce.' " I decide that I might as well get this topic out of the way, because it'll probably keep coming up. But I give her a look to let her know I'm on to her, in case there is something to be on to.

"It's important to share as many details and feelings as you can remember and feel comfortable sharing. You don't have to worry about my passing any judgments; just let it all hang out."

Ri-i-i-ght, lady; I'm just going to bare my soul to you after having known you for a week; I can't talk to my best friend or my mother about this, but I'm going to talk to you. Sure thing. "All right. Let me think. Okay. In second grade my friend MaryBeth's dad left his wife and four children for another man and moved to Connecticut. For a really long time I didn't know that he'd left with another *man*, because everyone in the family explained why he'd left by saying, 'He went to be gay.' I wasn't sure what that meant, or I didn't really think about it, I guess, until sixth grade . . . and then something just clicked when I was watching that TV show about a woman who one episode is dating guys and then one day decides she's a lesbian or whatever, and the show becomes a lesbian show?"

Lisz nods and looks a little confused.

"Anyway, I think that was my first experience with divorce."

I don't tell her how MaryBeth's dad never calls and seldom writes, how they never visit him in Connecticut, how when he actually remembers their birthdays he sends them a lame card with five dollars enclosed and tells them to spend it wisely, how MaryBeth's mom always looked so old and tired after he left, how she didn't do her hair or wear makeup for a long time. That kind of stuff hasn't happened to my family—not yet, at least—and I don't want Lisz to think I think my family is anything like that, so messed up and sad.

I also leave out how after her dad left, MaryBeth's family couldn't afford their house payment anymore, and they had to move to a smaller house in a dumpy neighborhood and lie about their address so they could still go to the schools in our district.

I forget to mention the fact that her family only recently

purchased a new car after driving a Buick that was old in second grade and was pretty disgusting nine years later. Nothing like that is going to happen to us. Things are barely going to change at all. I mean, we hardly ever saw my dad before, so his moving out isn't going to make a big difference.

"Is that all you want to say about that memory, that experience?" she asks.

"That's it."

"So, how do you think this experience has affected your perception of divorce?"

"What do you mean?"

"Do you feel that some of your fears or concerns about your parents' divorce are influenced at all by MaryBeth's family's story?"

"I don't think my father left us because of another man, if that's what you're asking."

I look at the clock. We still have thirty-five minutes left and I don't want to discuss my feelings about MaryBeth's gay dad, so I improvise. "Here's something interesting, though: last night I dreamed that my father and Mr. Bingler, my history teacher, made my family sit down on the couch because they had an announcement to make. They tap-danced and sang about how much they loved each other and then they told us about their plans to move to Connecticut. What do you think that means?"

"Well, I'm not really one for dream interpretation—"

I cut her off. "And I've had several dreams where my mother and Justin Timberlake run off together. But they always leave a note for us—very considerate of them, right?—talking about their great passion for each other and how they can't deny it any longer, stuff like that. Does that mean anything?"

I get her talking for a while about dreams, how not all of them mean something.

"Sometimes they are manifestations of our own fears and anxieties, or of our fantasies. You can't always find a literal interpretation, really. Sometimes they show what we're feeling at a certain point in our lives, and sometimes they're just a crazy jumble of nonsense," Lisz says.

Then she's back to MaryBeth's family's divorce.

"Do you think your parents' divorce will be like MaryBeth's?"

"I've never compared the two."

"I see. Well, that might be something to consider. Often our past experiences have an impact on the way we perceive and deal with new experiences."

"Hmmm. Okay. I'll think about that."

The hour is over.

Thinking about MaryBeth's family depresses me; it makes me feel like the world is covered in some kind of film, the way I used to feel after my grandmother took me to breakfast at this pancake house where the entire dining area seemed to be coated in maple syrup and bacon grease.

love means never having to eat your pepperoni

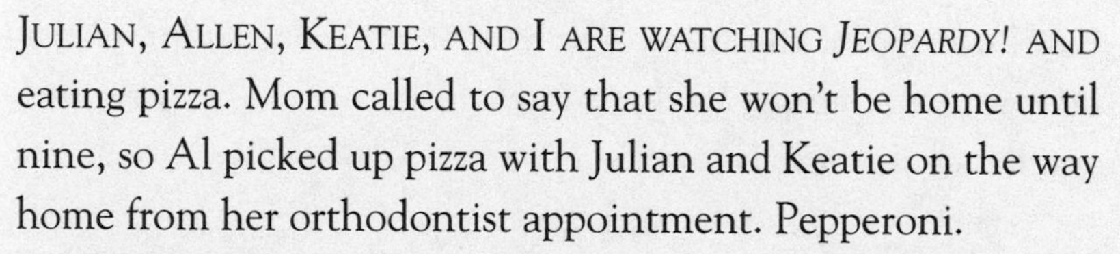

JULIAN, ALLEN, KEATIE, AND I ARE WATCHING *JEOPARDY!* AND eating pizza. Mom called to say that she won't be home until nine, so Al picked up pizza with Julian and Keatie on the way home from her orthodontist appointment. Pepperoni.

"What is Papua New Guinea?" Allen yells at the TV.

"Shouldn't the question be 'Where is Papua New Guinea?'" I tease.

"Shut up, smartass," Allen says. "I don't want to miss the next question."

"You want another piece, Meems?" Julian asks me.

"Sure." I pass my plate down the couch to him.

It takes him a while to pass it back. When Keatie hands me the plate, I notice that there's no pepperoni on the piece.

I hate eating pepperoni, but I like the way it makes pizza taste—the chewy, fatty, meatiness just grosses me out—so I always order pepperoni pizza and then pick off the pepperoni. That way I can still sort of taste the pepperoni, but I don't have to eat it.

I lean over and look down the couch to where Julian sits with a small stack of pepperoni on his plate, yelling out answers in the form of questions.

He's never touched my pepperoni before.

I want to frame this piece of pizza and hang it on my wall. I want to call Haley and tell her that Julian knows how I feel about pepperoni; he cares about my pepperoni needs, and he has met them.

But he isn't looking at me longingly while I eat my pizza or anything. . . .

If I were a seventeen-year-old guy with a stack of pepperoni on my lap and the girl who the pepperoni belonged to was sitting two cushions away from me on a sofa, what would I be feeling at this moment?

the forgotten fiddler

WHEN I LOOK AT MY PHONE AFTER DANCE PRACTICE, I HAVE three missed calls from Keatie. She has a cell phone she's only supposed to use in emergencies, so I'm kind of freaked out. I call her back without listening to the messages she's left.

"Mia?" Her voice is shaky, like she's crying. "Nobody came to get me. I finished violin and there's nobody here."

Keatie takes violin lessons at a music academy after school. There's this sort of cab service for kids that picks her up and takes her there, and then my mom, or sometimes Allen, picks her up. Since Mom started working more, she's had Allen pick Keatie up more often.

"Who was supposed to pick you up? Mom or Allen?"

"I don't remember. But nobody came. I've been waiting and waiting. I called Mommy and Daddy and Allen, but no one answers. I called them at work, too, but they said Daddy's showing property and Mom is with a client somewhere."

"Let me see if Ana and I can swing by the academy on our way home. Just a sec."

Ana has been half listening to my conversation while talking to some other girls and waiting for me. She nods when I look over at her.

"Yeah, Keatie, we'll come and get you, okay?"

"All right. I'll wait outside for you."

When we get to the academy, Keatie is sitting on the cement steps that lead to the entrance, hugging her violin case; her face is tearstained.

On the drive home, she cries a little when she tells us about how scared she was, how no one answered their phones, how long she waited. "Everyone forgot about me," she says. "No one remembered."

"I think they just got confused, Keat. They all thought someone else was taking care of you," I tell her, trying to convince both of us that that's what happened.

scorecard

SINCE DAD MOVED OUT, EVERYONE'S BEEN TALKING LESS. I counted the number of words I said to each of the members of my family today.

Allen: 43

Mom: 28

Keatie: 21

Dad: 11 (Not to him, exactly; to his answering machine.)

I don't really have any actual predivorce data to compare this to, but I can confidently hypothesize that we are talking less to each other. Much less. I can say this because my family has mysteriously developed a new language that is more efficient than any previously known to man. We have found a way to say as much as possible in as few words as possible. For example:

We used to greet each other by saying things like "Hey, Keatie, what's going on? How was your violin lesson?" or "Al, how's the bus? Have you gotten it to run without push-starting it yet?"

And then we'd talk about things, make fun of each other, make fun of Dad, make fun of Alex Trebek, or whatever.

Now our "conversations" go a little something like this:

"Hey," followed by a slight lifting of the chin.

To which the respondent often replies, "Erngh." Chin lift.

At the dinner table, we used to say things like "Please pass the tofu loaf" or "Are there any more rolls?"

Now we say, "Rolls." Or we just point at stuff.

We are like vaults now: just try and get an extra word out of us. I feel like maybe we could train CIA operatives in this language and make a fortune.

dial-a-dad

WHEN I WAS YOUNG, I FELT LIKE I NEEDED MY DAD. IN MY mind, he was a human encyclopedia. I'd call him at the drop of a hat.

"Hi, Dad. It's Mia. Do you have time to answer a question?"

"Hello, Mia. Actually, I'm with a client right now. . . ."

"But this'll be really fast. I promise. Allen says that Las Vegas is the capital of Nevada. But my teacher said it's Carson City, and my states and capitals test is tomorrow. . . ."

"It's Carson City, sweetie. Listen, I'll help you study when I get home tonight, okay?"

"Okay. Thanks."

I don't remember if he helped me study that night or not. But we could always count on him to know the answer to any homework question we ever had. Before he moved out, he seemed to answer his phone less and less, but now I can never seem to get ahold of him on the first try. Keatie's homework questions always go to Al or to me. She sees Dad as the guy who comes on vacations with us, to family parties, to dinner twice a week. I wonder if she has any idea how much he knows. It's like he's become a different dad.

soccer moms

ALLEN AND JULIAN ARE COACHING KEATIE'S SOCCER TEAM this season because none of the parents volunteered. Plus, they think it will look good on their college applications. They arrive home after the first practice talking and writing furiously on yellow legal pads. They sit down at the picnic table and don't seem to notice me working on my trig homework.

"Some of those kids suck," Allen says. "I mean, we've got some little champions, but that kid Mason? I thought he was going to kick himself in the head during drills."

"Yeah, and I thought Keatie was going to kick him in the head while they were scrimmaging, she was so mad that he couldn't dribble right," Julian says, laughing. "Either way, he needs some work." He scribbles something on his notepad.

"Keatie, Luis, and Chewy are the best players we've got. We're going to have to set every play up around them."

I start laughing.

"What?" Julian asks.

"You guys are acting like this is the NBA or NFL or something. . . . It's just a kids' soccer team."

Allen stares at me and takes a deep breath before he speaks, deliberately dramatic. "Listen, Mimoo. You like to dance. You spend hours in the basement making up *dances*. And then you go to competitions with your little friends to see who has the best dance. And sometimes you get all nervous and sweaty before you do your little dance." He turns to Julian. "Have you seen her do that, dude? It's pretty gross. Not attractive at all." Back to me. "Anyway, dancing is a helluva lot more ridiculous than soccer, and you get all worked up about that. And I have been nothing but supportive of your dancing, so I'd appreciate it if you'd show me the same courtesy."

"Supportive? Whatever. You know you've made fun of dance ever since I started."

"I have no idea what you're talking about," Allen says. "Back me up here, Julio."

"Sorry, Mia, I'm with Al. I have no recollection of ever making fun of dancing. Do you really get all sweaty before you compete?" Julian asks. "I'd like to see that."

He wants to see me sweat? What do these things mean?

"Sick. That was totally uncalled for, dude." Allen gives

Julian a look of confusion and disgust. He shakes his head. "Whatever. Dance, shmance. On to more important things: the team. We have no name."

"Right. So, what do you think we should call ourselves?" Julian asks me.

"How about something that uses your and Al's names? Like the . . . um, Woody Jewels or something?" I suggest.

"Are you kidding me? That sounds like the name of a porn movie or something," Allen says.

"Everything is sex to you," I say. "What about the Sharks?"

"Okay, that's good. But why sharks? What about our team makes them *sharks?*" Julian asks.

"I don't know." I cannot believe they're this serious about anything. "Does the name have to mean something?"

"Hey, what if we do a Yorba Linda–themed name," Allen says. "Like the Nixons? Or the Fighting Oranges? What about Yorba United? Like Manchester United, you know?"

"That's a possibility," Julian says. "Write that down."

"I need to do my homework; can you guys go somewhere else?" I ask.

Allen and Julian decide to move their meeting to the basement. A few minutes later Julian returns.

"Hey, um, I didn't mean to shoot you down about the Sharks. I mean, that was a cool name."

"No worries. I don't really care what you guys name the team. It's none of my business anyway."

"Yeah. Okay. Just making sure. See you later," he says, looking at me kind of weird before going back to the basement.

First the pepperoni, then the sweat, now the apology. Julian is definitely acting strange. With all the changes going on around here, is it possible that one of them is actually good? What if Julian is different? What if he thinks I'm different? What if, amidst the absolute and total annihilation of my family, Julian Paynter has decided he likes me? Just when I have basically gone completely crazy? Or maybe it's the craziness that's making me think he likes me. Should I say something? Start lying out in a bikini in the front yard?

WHENEVER YOU'RE MARKED ABSENT FROM A CLASS AT MY school, you get a call from the school district that night, a recorded voice that says:

"According to our records, your child missed one or more classes today. Please contact your school attendance office regarding this absence."

Today is the third day in a row I've answered the phone and heard the recording. I haven't missed a single class. And I always drive to school with Allen, so I know he's there. At least, he's there at some point. . . . The last thing this family needs is a delinquent kid.

I tell my mom to call the attendance office about the mistakes they've been making.

prom date

↕

Julian comes over and Allen isn't around. I'm watching MTV on the couch, and Julian sits down next to me, grabs the remote, and turns off the TV.

"What's going on with you?" he asks.

"What do you mean?" I ask, staring at the blank screen.

"Do you, um, need someone to talk to . . . about anything?"

"So you and Allen have decided to compete for the role of replacement parent, then," I say.

"What's that supposed to mean? You're acting like a zombie. And . . . well, you don't stare at me the way you used to. What's going on?"

Has he noticed how I look at him? Great. Has it really changed or is he just talking crazy? Since when does Julian notice the way I look at him? Since when does he talk crazy? "The sky is falling. Nine models wore leg warmers in the last issue of *Seventeen*."

"That's, uh, too bad." He's acting weird again; he's sitting up too straight. "Did you know that prom is on a Saturday this year?" he asks. What does prom have to do with leg warmers?

"It's on a Saturday every year," I tell him. "Who cares?"

"So, do you wanna go or what?" Julian asks.

I turn to see if he's being serious; he's staring at the blank TV screen now. He looks pained, as if he's watching someone die rather than staring at an empty gray box.

"Very funny."

"I'm serious."

"What? Did Allen tell you to ask me because he thinks I'm depressed or something? Are you asking me because you feel sorry for me? And isn't prom like seven years away?"

"Mia, I don't feel sorry for you. Well, I do if you really think leg warmers are a big deal. . . . But Allen didn't tell me to ask you. In fact, he'd probably get mad at me and tell me to keep my hands off you if he knew I was asking you." He pauses and waits for me to say something.

I can't breathe. I can't speak. I mean, I have been preparing for this moment for my entire conscious existence, and I somehow have no idea what to say or do.

Julian continues, "I want to go with you. And I wanted to ask you before anyone else did."

For some reason, I start staring at the TV again, too; maybe that's what I'm supposed to do and Julian is trying to show me, so I don't get it wrong. . . . Or not . . . "If this is a joke, I will kill you."

"Can't you make this even a little bit easy? What do I have to do? Get down on one knee?" He stops staring at the TV and looks at me. "C'mon, Meezer."

I want to shout, "Of course I'll go. I love you. I want to bear your children. I would go snorkeling in a pit of nuclear waste with you if you asked me to." Instead, I say, "Fine, Julian, I'll go, but only because you begged and because I needed an excuse to buy some silver leg warmers." Brilliant. Now he probably thinks I hate him.

"Good." He smiles and looks relieved for a second, but only a second. "Now I have to figure out what to tell your brother."

So what if in ten years global warming is going to make the ice caps melt and flood the planet and kill off the entire human population? Who cares if my family thinks it's okay to spontaneously combust? I get to think happy thoughts and live in an alternate universe, one where Julian Paynter and I live on love and stare into each other's eyes all day between make-outs. That will be my future. Everyone else can wallow in misery. I am a princess; my fairy tale has finally begun.

best friend?

HALEY ANSWERS THE PHONE ON THE THIRD RING. "HEY, stranger."

"He asked me," I tell her.

"Great. Congratulations," she replies. "Who asked you what?"

"Julian. To the prom."

"Are you serious? What happened? How? What's been going on with you guys? Is this why you've been so hard to get ahold of lately? I can't believe you didn't tell me. I can't believe this."

"I did tell you. I mean, I *am* telling you. Nothing's been going on. I mean, he's been acting weird, but the prom thing kind of came outta nowhere." I start to wonder how long it's been since I've talked to Haley about anything real, anything important. Before I can stop myself I tell her, "My dad moved out."

"Oh, Meems. Shit. I'm sorry. When? I wish I'd known. I would've come over or you could've come over here . . . to talk about it . . . or something."

I am so tired of trying not to think about them or talk about them. I am tired of spending my life trying to figure out what happened to my parents and what I'm supposed to do about it, and hiding it from everyone so that when whatever is wrong is right again no one will be the wiser. I am tired of avoiding feeling sad by feeling numb. And I get cold inside when I think about talking about it. I want to talk about Julian and dresses and how pissed Kiki Nordgren will be when she finds out.

"I don't know," I tell Haley. "I don't know what to say about it. I would have told you, but there was never really a good time to bring it up. It happened so fast, you know."

I couldn't explain to Haley what had been happening because I didn't really know. I felt retarded for not telling her, and for having a messed-up family. And it's not like it happened all at once, either; it had been happening for a long time. But how do you tell your best friend that there are a million things you never said and that there will probably be a million more? If there are things I couldn't even admit to myself, how could I have told Haley about them, best friend or not? Realizing that, I wonder what I really know about Haley and her family—whether everyone keeps so much hidden.

Haley's dad sleeps in the living room on the couch, but

supposedly that's because he has really bad gas problems or something; it's nothing to do with the state of her parents' marriage.

"Hey, listen, I've gotta go now. My dad's here. We're all going out to dinner together," I lie, to get off the phone.

"Well, call me when you get back. I want to talk to you."

"I will. Bye."

"See ya."

Why is it that even when something great happens, the bad stuff taints it? Why can't I tell Haley about Julian without talking about my parents? Why can't I keep those things separate? I just need to be more careful, I guess. How can I ever feel happy if all the painful and sad things keep leaking into the good ones?

impulse

TWO YEARS AGO, WHEN WE WERE ON VACATION IN ARIZONA, my mom found out that a car auction was being held near our hotel. She's not really a car aficionado, but for some reason she fell in love with this car there, and when no one bid on it, she approached the owner as he was loading it onto the truck with the other cars that hadn't sold. She negotiated a price, bought it, and drove it back to the hotel to show us. Dad was livid, and he said it was because she hadn't discussed it with him first and she hadn't done any research on the car. Mom suggested that maybe he was angry because she had a vintage red Porsche and he didn't, which only made him angrier. They got like that sometimes. They clashed. They had such different ways of doing things. Usually they complemented each other: Mom's impulsiveness eased Dad's rigidness; Dad's careful way of doing things saved some of Mom's not-so-well-thought-out plans from being total disasters. But sometimes, like with the car, they were both too stubborn to compromise, and the battles ended with each of them doing what they thought was right. This time was like that.

Mom and I drove the car home, across desert highways; through orange groves, strawberry fields, and suburban neighborhoods; right into our driveway, while Dad, Allen, Julian, and Keatie took a plane back. Mom kept the top down most of the way and told me stories about her first car, the first new car she and Dad had ever owned. I told her about my dream car, sang along to songs on the classic-rock radio station, felt like I was free, somehow.

That's how it was with us. She would listen to me talk about anything; she told me stories about what she was like when she was my age. I wasn't afraid of my mom, the way some kids are of theirs. I always felt like she understood me. Like she liked me. Like she liked being my mom. Lately, though, whenever I want to talk to her, I feel like I'm interrupting something. Like it isn't fun for her anymore. Like I'm a burden.

life imitates art

ONE SATURDAY NIGHT AFTER DAD'S BEEN GONE A FEW WEEKS, Mom asks me if I want to go to the movies with her, just the two of us, since Allen is at work and Keatie is at Dad's.

"Sure," I say.

The movie is the only one showing at a theater that people are always trying to shut down because it's old and ugly. It shows movies that are kind of old, but not really old; they're not black-and-white or anything. The one we see is kind of depressing. It's about all these people who just kind of fall into a coma for no apparent reason, just kind of check out of life one day. Then this doctor finds a medicine that seems to wake them up and the people start to live and talk and act normal, but eventually the medicine stops working and the people go back to their coma. Mom and I both cry at the end when all the people are lined up, listless, in their hospital beds again.

We drive home in her car, listening to a Righteous Brothers CD. She begins to tell me about Dad. About them.

"When we started dating, my friends thought I was crazy. We didn't have anything in common, really. Your father was interested in politics and philosophy; I couldn't have cared less about those things . . . but he was so smart, and he just *adored* me. And it seemed as if, ultimately, we wanted the same things—family, a home, a life together. . . ."

"No offense, Mom, but, duh . . . everyone wants those things. So you married Dad because he liked you and because he wanted to live in a house and have kids?"

"That's not what everyone wants, actually, Mia. Julian's dad didn't want those things, and it seems that your dad didn't, either. A few years after Keatie was born, he became distant. He started working longer hours; he seemed less interested in me, in you kids, in being a husband and a father. It was as if he just slipped away. Even when he was present physically, he seemed absent, like his mind, maybe his heart, was somewhere else."

What she's telling me makes me uncomfortable. How could someone be in one place and be someplace else at the same time? How come I had never noticed what my mom was talking about? "What do you mean?"

"He just became . . . vacant, empty. I don't quite know how to explain it. He just checked out on us. But then after a while, he'd be back just like he was before—happy . . . alive. . . . Those times made me think we would be okay.

Every time he went back to his old self, I told myself he was back for good, that the . . . emotional absence had just been a phase. I'm sorry, Mia, I shouldn't be telling you all this," she apologizes. But she goes on anyway. "The times when he was involved and excited and loving were so wonderful, but then he'd check out again. Kind of like the people in the movie. It became a sort of bittersweet cycle. . . . We tried therapy, but your father . . . It's hard being married to a ghost."

I have no idea what she means, how my father, who has always lived in the same house as us, living, breathing, working, was ever like any of the people in the movie—absent, empty, unresponsive.

I nod anyway. It feels like she needs that.

"But he kept falling back asleep, kept going back to it."

"Yeah." I nod again, wonder who my father is when he isn't just my dad, the guy who helps me with my math homework and talks about Woody Allen. He is someone who grew up, who had dreams, who maybe lost them, who feels things; someone who became a ghost to my mother while he still seemed real, unchanging, to me, his daughter. I think of how I've sometimes felt like I'm watching my life pass by, like I'm watching a movie, and I wonder if I am like him. The back of my throat aches; my chest feels like it's being pumped full of Jell-O. I suddenly feel as if I have to concentrate just to breathe. I can't remember ever having felt as scared as I do now.

The song "Little Latin Lupe Lu" begins to play. We have to sing along. It's what we always do.

"Did I ever tell you that the Righteous Brothers used to

practice in my neighbors' garage? My mom used to take us down to listen to them," Mom says.

I remember. She's told me a thousand times before. Every time we listen to the CD. I remember how the first boy she ever kissed, Tony Rojas, when she was in seventh grade, told her not to tell anyone they'd made out because he didn't want the other girls to think he was her boyfriend.

"Julian asked me to go to the prom with him," I tell her.

"That's wonderful, sweetie," she says, instantly my mom again. "When did he ask you? What did he say? What did Allen say?"

We talk about proms, high school, boyfriends, the whole way home. But it feels different. I know she is hurt and confused and scared. I guess I've known that for a while, but I've tried to ignore it. And now I can't. How will she hold us all together, keep us all afloat? How will she rescue us if her boat is sinking, too?

Tonight I can't sleep. I keep thinking about the things Mom said. I can't make sense of them. Why didn't I ever see my dad the way my mom did? If he was acting so weird, if there were times when he didn't want to be with us, didn't care about us, why didn't I see them? I wonder if maybe he and Mom would have been okay if they hadn't had kids, if he'd been able to make his films or be a philosopher or do whatever he wanted to do. I wonder what my dad thinks of me, how he feels about me. I mean, I know he must love me; I'm his kid. But does he like me? Does he think I stole his life? Does he blame me for his lost dreams?

documentary

↕

I FIND KEATIE WATCHING OUR FAMILY MOVIES—VIDEOTAPES of dance recitals, vacations, birthday parties, Christmas mornings, Easter egg hunts, championship soccer games—when I go down to the basement to practice my new routine. I notice that she keeps watching the same part of one tape over and over again; I think it must've been made on the first day we had the new camera.

In the scene Keatie watches, Dad wants to make sure the camera works, so he wanders around the house taping, droning on about whose room is where and how long we've lived in the house, until Keatie convinces him to let her hold the camera. She has a hard time keeping the camera steady as she zooms in on my parents in the kitchen.

Mom unloads groceries, unaware that Dad is sneaking up behind her until he blows on the back of her neck.

Mom turns around and laughs. "What on earth are you doing?" She and Dad kiss.

Keatie's disembodied voice is heard: "Do it again!" And they do. You can hear Keatie giggling. Mom puts her hand in front of the camera lens and the screen goes dark.

"Keatie, why do you keep watching that part of the movie?" I ask her as I lift one leg onto the barre to stretch.

"What part?" she asks.

"You know which part. The one you keep rewinding to."

She watches the scene again and doesn't answer until it's over and the tape is rewinding again. "I like it because I got to hold the camera."

It makes sense. She was in charge, and when she was, they were happy. And now all she can do is watch—a person passing the scene of the accident.

a new dance

WHEN I FIRST DECIDED I WANTED TO MAKE UP MY OWN dances, all the choreography I did had a pattern. I'd start with slow, balletic combinations; then I'd gradually push into something faster, with more hip-hop and jazz steps; then I'd morph into slow movements again, winding down until I stopped. I always thought about how my legs and feet moved and planned that out before I considered how my hands and arms would go. One of my dance teachers pointed it out and worked with me on "expanding" my style of choreography; if she hadn't, I'd still be doing variations of the same dance.

"How has your week been?" Lisz asks.

"Good."

I realize we are doing the same dance every week, Lisz and I. She asks me questions that I don't like, and I give her answers that don't seem to do much for her. But I can't stop moving in the same direction, with the same steps I've been using. I feel stuck. I am too afraid to move forward; every time I try, things get so difficult, nothing feels safe.

"Anything you want to discuss?" she asks, with the same level of belief and anticipation and expectation she always has, as if she knows I will crack eventually.

"Yeah. There's actually a lot I want to discuss."

"Really?" She isn't as surprised as I'd like her to be.

"Yeah, but I don't understand what good it would do me to talk to you. Or to talk at all. How will sitting here talking change anything?"

Now she seems surprised. I want her to be speechless. Or to tell me that I'm right.

"What is it that you want to change, Mia?"

As if there is music playing in my brain, I feel myself following a familiar pattern, snapping back into position.

"My hair color, maybe. Maybe if I were blond, my life would be more interesting."

"Perhaps, but is that the only element of your life you'd like to alter? What else would you like to change?"

I think about my mom, how fragile she seemed when she tried to talk to me about my dad; about the phone calls from the school and how I hardly ever see Allen at lunch; about Keatie watching the same thing over and over again. I think about myself. I am normal. I am not falling apart the way they are. "I really just want to play spit. Can we do that?"

"You're close, Mia. I know that you understand and see a

lot more than you want to admit. I think those things weigh on you. I think that talking about them will help you to feel less burdened. Can we talk about those things?"

My throat itches; my jaw tightens.

"I don't know what I see. Maybe I don't see anything," I tell her as I pick up a deck of cards and begin to shuffle.

daddy-daughter date

My church has weekly activities for "the youth," so that we don't turn into delinquents. You know, they want us to have things to do besides smoke pot, shoplift, and have sex, so they have these activities. When I was ten, they planned this thing called the Daddy-Daughter Date for all the ten- and eleven-year-old girls and their dads. I think they had it for the younger girls because by the time you get to junior high and especially high school, there's no way you'd want to go on a date with your dad. Anyway, it was a big deal because my dad worked all the time and was seldom home before ten or eleven o'clock most nights, but he promised me that he was going to come home early especially for my Daddy-Daughter Date.

I tried on every nice dress and skirt I owned and asked Allen a thousand times which one I should wear.

"Everything looks fine until *you* put it on," he said.

"I'm serious," I said, "I want to look nice. It's important. It's for my Daddy-Daughter Date."

"Wear that black one, then. Aren't you embarrassed to be going on a date with *Dad*?"

"No. Because he's smarter than everyone else's dad and we're having games, so I know we'll win."

Allen snickered. "Whatever."

The Daddy-Daughter Date started at six-thirty. We'd made invitations and given them out weeks before, so I was sure Dad knew what time we were supposed to be there. Mom did my hair in a French braid, and by six o'clock I was ready to go. I sat stiffly on the couch in the living room, so that my hair and dress wouldn't get messed up, and I watched TV. By six-twenty, I was getting nervous. I called Dad's office to see when he'd left, but the night secretary didn't know. So I continued to wait.

Dad arrived breathless at six-forty.

"Dad, we're late," I said, "let's go."

"Mia, I need to take a shower and change, I've been in these clothes all day."

"But Da-ad . . ."

"I'll be ready in five minutes."

I stood outside the bathroom door while my dad showered, shouting instructions at him.

"They're having these games to see how well we know each other, so I am going to tell you things about me, and you have to remember them."

No response.

"Okay?" I screamed.

"Okay," Dad yelled back.

"My favorite color is lavender. My favorite singer is . . ."

I gave him an impossible amount of information to remember, but when I quizzed him, he got almost all the answers right.

Dad wore a tuxedo on our date. I felt so grown-up and important. We were pretty late to the dinner, but the games didn't start until after we arrived. There were three games; we won two.

When we drove home, my dad said, "You look lovely, Mia, did I mention that earlier? You were the smartest, most beautiful girl in the room."

"Thanks, Dad. You did a really good job on the games. Thanks for coming."

At the next stoplight, he leaned over and kissed the top of my head and patted my shoulder.

Dad bought me a green sweater for my eleventh birthday; I guess by then he'd forgotten my favorite color.

Thinking about it now, I can't help wondering about what my mom told me about my dad's slipping away/being a ghost. I feel like my dad was definitely there with me that night. All of him.

the bathrobe incident

I'M LATE GETTING READY FOR SCHOOL, AND ALLEN LEAVES without me, without telling me. He's never done that before, but then again, we have entered an era of doing all kinds of stuff we've never done before. I guess he assumes that I can get a ride to school with Haley. But I can't; she's already at school for tennis practice. Mom's already at work, so I call and ask Dad to take me. He sounds sleepy when he answers the phone.

"I'll be there in five minutes. Wait out in front."

I wait. Twenty minutes later, five minutes into first period, Dad drives up frantically. In a bathrobe. The old blue bathrobe he's worn every morning since before I can remember. I say "before I can remember" because I have seen pictures of my father holding me when I was a baby, and in them he is wearing that blue robe. But he's never worn the bathrobe outside our house before. Okay, I mean, he's walked out to the end of the driveway to pick up the newspaper, but that's as far as he's gone. He's never *driven* anywhere in the bathrobe. In fact, he used to get mad if we wore our pajamas after ten a.m. on weekends. "I am not raising lazy, undressed sloths," he'd say.

"Get in," he shouts, throwing the door of the car open.

I manage to jump in before he speeds off. I worry the whole way to school that we are going to die or get pulled over by the police. Dad doesn't say anything about the bathrobe during our drive, he just sings along loudly with the opera playing on the radio. When we arrive at school, he leans over me to open my door.

"Have a good day," he sings.

"Thanks for the ride," I say.

"Yup. No problem. Listen, I don't know if I mentioned this before, but I'm leaving for Peru tomorrow. I'll be gone for two weeks, so if something like this happens again, I may not be around to help."

"What do you mean you're leaving for Peru? For business?" Since when does my dad take vacations without us? Since when does he take off from work for two whole weeks?

"I joined a hiking club. We're doing the Inca Trail."

"Oh." I am too shocked to say more.

"Take care, sweetie. And would you mind telling your brother and sister, in case I don't get a chance to? And your mother—" He catches himself before he can finish. "Have a good day at school."

And he drives off.

It's strange the way sometimes your life feels like a sitcom or a movie. Like you are watching it but not really living it. Like it's too bizarre or too clichéd to be real. My parents are separated, probably getting a divorce, so my older brother sometimes acts like he's my father, or like he's a mysterious superhero or criminal, and my little sister thinks nothing out of the ordinary is going on—maybe she's just pretending, too, who knows. It seems like a case study from a self-help book, or an episode of the Dr. Phil show—clichéd. My father driving me to school in a bathrobe, like bathwear has suddenly come into fashion or something, that's bizarre.

I breathe deeply and walk into my history class, expecting some kind of reprimand for being late, but my teacher is too absorbed in what he's saying to comment. He just nods at my seat and keeps talking.

"Many of our founding fathers had venereal diseases, the most common being syphilis. They weren't the paragons of morality and virtue your books would have you believe they were, at least not in the sense the book implies. They were powerful men of vision, but they were human nonetheless. . . ." Mr. Bingler lectures nonstop for the rest of the period, attempting to dispel all the myths surrounding Colonial American history and various "truths" and myths about half of the presidents since then. I try not to listen. I try not to think about the flaws we discover in people we thought we could count on. It's so much easier to keep things flat and simple, to live in a myth or a fairy tale. Your body can only digest so much new "truth" and information in a day. Being driven to school by a lunatic in a bathrobe who claims to be my father and learning that fat old Ben Franklin, who I've thought of since third grade as the guy with the kite and the key who discovered electricity, was some kind of lady-killer with an STD are already more than I can stomach. I feel like I am going to cry or faint or go completely crazy—start talking to myself or forgetting to put on key articles of clothing before I leave the house. When the laws of the universe all stop working but the world keeps spinning, how do you keep your balance? How do you stop yourself from falling, from flying into oblivion?

At lunch, I look for Allen, but I don't see him anywhere. His pea green VW bus, which is usually conspicuous in a parking lot full of SUVs and three-year-old BMWs, is nowhere to be seen.

mirror image

↕

I REMEMBER WHAT HALEY SAID ABOUT THE FREAK BATHROOMS, the ones none of our friends ever use. Maybe I'm one of the freaks now; maybe I've been one all along. I decide to use one of them, the one in the math building—don't get me wrong, I'm curious about industrial technology, but I've got to pace myself. When I walk through the door, it's like walking into one of those old movies from the eighties about high school, the ones that show girls with too much makeup on smoking in the bathroom while they try to hide their hickeys with cheap cover-up and talk about abortions. Well, it's almost like that. It smells like smoke and there're trashy girls. I rush into an empty stall. While I sit there—too nervous to pee, for some reason—I listen to them talk.

"I had to call into work for her this morning because

she was too wasted to get out of bed. I told them it was food poisoning."

"They believe you?"

"Who knows. They acted like they did. They have to. Who else are they gonna find to work that crap job?"

I sit in the stall, not quite understanding what I'm doing there, trying to breathe, when I find myself in tears. Not just crying quietly, but sobbing, unable to catch my breath, making loud gulping sounds. I haven't cried like this since I broke my femur in a freak trampoline accident. The bathroom goes silent except for my wailing. I imagine the girls looking at each other, trying to figure out who's in here, what's going on. The second-period "bell" sounds, an unnatural electronic buzz.

"Shit. If I'm marked late again, they'll call my house."

I wait in the stall until I hear them leave. When everything is quiet, I unlatch the door and walk over to the sink. I've started to wash my hands, just because it seems gross to leave a bathroom without washing your hands, when I hear a retching sound. Someone is throwing up. I freeze. The toilet flushes and I hear the sound of a door being unlatched. Without thinking, I turn around to look at the puker. It's Kiki Nordgren. She doesn't belong in this bathroom. And she doesn't look sick, the way you should if you've just thrown up.

I realize I'm staring. I push down the handle of the towel machine and the grating sound reverberates through the bathroom. I dry my hands, looking back once more before I push through the door; she is watching me.

After school I see Kiki walking to her car with a few of her bratty friends. She looks perfectly healthy. So if she wasn't throwing up because she was sick . . .

So even Kiki . . .

It seems impossible.

green-eyed monster

↕

He calls me up, whispering, "Okay, he's here, and I'm going to tell him, but I wanted to tell you first . . . that I am going to tell him . . . so that you know."

"Who is this?" I ask.

"Cute. Very cute," Julian is still whispering.

"Why are you whispering?" I yell into the phone. I get giddy like this whenever we interact now; I start acting crazy and silly, and I instinctively start bouncing on the balls of my feet. I am trying to learn to rein it in. Usually it takes a good three to five minutes for me to be able to act and communicate like a normal person. Julian is surprisingly normal about my weirdness. But now that I think about it, he usually seems kind of nervous, too, so maybe he doesn't notice how weird I act.

He begins to speak in his regular tone of voice. "Allen is here and I'm going to tell him that I asked you. . . ."

"Is it really that big a deal?" I whisper, trying to throw him off.

"I don't know," he starts to whisper again, but catches himself. "Quit doing that—the loud and then the whispering. Listen, I just wanted to warn you in case he freaks out and we have to . . . flee . . . or something."

"Flee? Did you just say 'flee'? Why are you talking like a spy? And where would we go? . . . We can't flee. . . ."

I hear Allen's voice in the background.

"Who are you talking to? Are you *whispering*?"

"Listen," Julian says, "I gotta go. Bye." He hangs up the phone.

I call him right back. He answers on the first ring.

"What," he says, "you think I shouldn't tell him?"

"The marshmallow floats at midnight," I whisper, and hang up.

Allen walks through the door twenty minutes later. "Has he, like, ummm, touched you or anything?" he asks.

"I wish," I tell him.

"Gross," he says. "At least it's not Kiki, though. I told Julian, 'Mia's weird and whatever, but at least she's not all *intense* like Kiki.' "

"Thanks for your support."

I find myself humming Broadway show tunes and making up lyrics in my head about how the world knows I'm in love and my brother doesn't think I'm too intense.

the end of an era

"WHAT ARE WE GOING TO EAT TONIGHT?" KEATIE ASKS. "IT'S date night. I want Chinese."

"Date night?"

I'm confused for a moment about who she's referring to, what she means, and I remember. She thinks my parents are going out like they used to, even though Dad moved out.

"I don't think they're going on dates anymore, Keat."

"Why? They especially need dates now so that they can see each other and fall in love."

Well, anyway, Dad's in Peru. I can't figure out if Keatie is trying to change what has happened or if she just can't see what has changed.

showdown

On the days when I don't have dance class during school, I typically have practice either before or after school, which means that I usually get to see Kiki Nordgren five days of every week. At these practices, Kiki typically does one of the following three things:

(1) ignores me.

(2) talks about whoever she's dating in front of me—probably hoping that I'll talk to Allen about it.

(3) tries to rechoreograph my routines.

After seeing her in the outcast bathroom, I assumed this would change; I thought maybe Kiki would be nicer to me, so that I wouldn't say anything, or that she'd be even meaner to me because I'd discovered her secret. Truthfully, I hoped she would change somehow, become a nicer person because she had problems or something. Yeah, right.

At first she was a little different. She still did all the stuff she normally did, but it felt a little forced, kind of awkward. After a few practices, after I didn't say or do anything about what I'd seen, Kiki was her old self again.

I guess a lot of people started getting asked to the prom around the time Julian asked me, because today at our after-school practice, everyone is talking about the prom. I am friends with most of the girls on the team; some are members of Kiki's legion of brats, but for the most part, the other girls don't really care whether I convinced my brother to break up with Kiki or whether Kiki likes me. Most of them can't remember who was dating who six weeks ago, much less six months ago.

While we stretch, everyone talks. Mandy has been asked by a guy she doesn't really want to go with; Ana hasn't been asked at all, but Ben, the guy she has a crush on, hasn't asked anyone yet, so she's hoping she still has a chance. I'm dying to tell the entire planet that I'm going to the prom with Julian. I told Mandy and Ana at practice two days after Julian asked me, but no one else knows; I am sort of waiting my turn, waiting for someone to ask me whether I've been asked.

Kiki Nordgren doesn't have to wait.

"Kiki, who's asked you so far?" a sophomore in the Cult of Kiki wants to know.

I hate the way people just assume that more than one guy will ask Kiki.

"Jake Dowdle and Ryan Walker," she says. She manages to sound bored by the whole conversation.

I hate that she *has* been asked by more than one guy.

"Are you going to say yes to either of them?" Mandy asks.

"I don't think so. I'm waiting for someone else to ask me."

"Who?" half the team choruses, probably worried that Kiki has set her sights on their potential prom dates.

"I'm pretty sure Julian Paynter is going to ask me, and I'm going to go with him," Kiki says, glancing back at me. She leans forward, acting like she's letting the girls in on a big secret, like they have all suddenly become her confidantes. "I think the whole reason Allen and I had problems is because Julian liked me so much. Allen probably didn't know it until after we started dating because Julian was too shy to say anything. So when Allen found out, he broke up with me, for Julian's sake. Plus, Allen's probably gay anyway; I think he was using me as a beard or something."

A few of the girls laugh when she says this.

Kiki speaks as if there's no doubt that what she said is true. I freeze. I know I need to do something, but all I can think of involves running at her, screaming, jumping on her back, and clawing at her perfect face. I could ask Kiki if her lunches taste as good coming up as they do going down. I could tell everyone what I heard in the bathroom. I could spread rumors about her, the way she always does about me, make her look ridiculous for once. But I am frozen. And even if I weren't, I don't know if I could expose Kiki.

Ana speaks before I can, though. "Kiki, Julian already has a date. He's going with Mia. He asked her a while ago. Right, Meems?"

Every girl in the room turns to stare at me.

"Yeah. He did." This is my chance to tell it like it is, to get Kiki back for all the lies she's told, all the rumors and mean things I know she's said about me. "And my brother isn't gay." Beautiful. Way to stick it to her. That'll show her, Mia.

For a moment, Kiki looks scared and embarrassed, but in a millisecond her face has turned back to stone. When she speaks, her voice is even. "I think I'd be a better judge of that than you would, sweetie. How nice of Julian to ask you. He must really be looking out for you . . . with everything that's been going on with your family and all."

How does Kiki know anything about my family? I am too stunned to say anything.

Ana comes to my rescue. "Is that why guys ask girls to prom, then, Kiki? And you've been asked twice already?"

The ability to be catty and cruel must be genetic; I've watched enough reality television, talk shows, and soap operas to have picked it up by now if it's a skill you can learn, but I can't think of anything to say. I'm outmatched.

"I think I forgot my water bottle," I say as I retreat.

In the girls' locker room, I imagine what I could have said to Kiki, how I could have won. I think about my mother, how she stayed in her room all day when my father left, even though she had asked him to leave. Maybe I've inherited more than just her nose and eyes.

greek to me

WHEN I WAS FOUR YEARS OLD, MY DAD SPENT AN ENTIRE afternoon trying to teach me the Greek alphabet. He was reading an old book in Greek for graduate school; I asked him what it was, and he decided to teach me the Greek alphabet. He taught it to me as a song, to the tune of "Twinkle, Twinkle, Little Star," and we sang it together to my mom and Allen that night. I only remember the first four letters now, but I remember clearly how it felt to hold Dad's hand and sing.

special friends

My dad e-mailed us from Peru to tell us he had a surprise for us and that he wanted us all to meet for dinner the night after he got back.

"Maybe he bought me a llama. I Googled Peru and it said a lot about llamas. I saw some pictures. Llamas look like a cross between camels and ponies . . . and ostriches," Keatie says as we drive to the restaurant.

Allen laughs. "I doubt he bought you a llama, Keater. He probably brought us a bunch of hideous sweaters, and I bet his surprise is something like he wants to take us all to Peru this summer. If we're lucky it'll be that he wants to move there."

Since Dad moved out, he has ignored Al. I mean, we've all seen a decline in Dad-attention, except for Keatie, maybe, who insists on having daily conversations with my dad about anything she can think of just so she can keep him on the phone, but it's worse with Al and Dad. They always had trouble getting along before, but now it's like they're having some kind of silent face-off.

"Prepare to be llama-fied," Al tells us when we arrive at the restaurant.

Allen steels his face when we get out of the car. He looks like he's about to be tortured by terrorists looking for government secrets.

We tell the hostess we're supposed to meet my dad.

"Right," she says. "They're waiting for you. Follow me, please."

I don't understand why she said "they" until I see the table she is leading us to. My dad, tanner than normal, is talking to a woman sitting next to him at the table.

Dad stands when he sees us. "Kids . . . hello. Good to see you." He takes the woman's hand and she stands up. "This is Paloma." He acts as if this should mean something to us.

We stand there, quiet.

She reaches toward us to shake our hands. "I am Paloma. Of Peru."

Keatie takes her hand and shakes it limply.

I put my hand out to shake Paloma's; Al shoves his in his pocket.

Dads glowers at Al and gestures toward the table. "Well, come on, have a seat. Let's order."

We slowly take our seats. Keatie insists on sitting next to my dad, wedging herself in between him and the Peruvian, who I end up sitting next to. She smiles hopefully at me, and I smile wanly back. Allen sits next to me.

"Why is she here?" Keatie asks as soon as she is seated. "Is she going to clean your apartment?"

I lower my head in embarrassment and hope that this woman doesn't speak English very well.

Keatie's limited experience with Hispanic women has been her close association with our Latin American housekeepers, who also sort of acted as babysitters to her. Now that we're all old enough to watch and clean up after ourselves, we don't have a housekeeper. Anyway, none of them were anything like Paloma. They were all kind of round and motherly; not Paloma—she's wearing a tight black minidress and strappy high-heeled shoes. I wonder where Dad found her, and if she hiked around the jungle in outfits like that.

"Paloma is, uh, my, ummm, my new special friend," Dad stammers.

"What do you need a special friend for? You don't even have time to play with us," Keatie reminds him.

Allen and I look at each other and smirk. No one is going to give Dad any help on this one.

"Yeah, Dad, what are you going to do with a special friend?" Allen asks.

Dad says something about how Paloma showed him her country and now he is going to show her his.

"So it was kind of this thing where you were like, 'Hey,

Paloma, you show me yours, I'll show you mine.' Something like that, Dad?" I try to sound like I am genuinely trying to help him out.

Dad ignores me.

At that moment everyone at the table looks in Paloma's direction to see her reaction to the argument that centers around her. She is applying lipstick and looking into the mirror of her compact but quickly puts the stuff away when she realizes that our conversation has ground to a halt.

"Sorry," she says, her accent thick. "Everything okay?" she asks, smiling, trying to figure out what to say.

"So she *does* speak English," I say aloud, before I can catch myself.

Before Dad can say anything, Allen is on his feet. "I gotta go."

I stand up. "Yeah, me too. Early-morning practice."

Keatie looks confused. I try to motion toward the door with my head.

"What?" she asks.

"Do you want to stay or go?" I try not to sound mean.

"Go, I guess." She looks like she is about to cry as she gets up from the table. "But we didn't even eat. And Dad has surprises."

"If he has any more surprises, I'm sure he'll bring them over later," Allen says, putting his hands on Keatie's shoulders and turning her in the direction of the restaurant's entrance. "We can eat at Wendy's."

Although Keatie could eat nothing but chicken nuggets

for the rest of her life and die happy, she doesn't quite accept this bribe the way she normally would. Once she's gotten her nuggets, she eats only one and a half before handing the box to me and telling me she's full.

I nibble on my bacon cheeseburger even though I'm not hungry, either.

When we get home, Keatie tells my mom about Paloma. "Daddy made a friend named Paloma in Peru and now she's visiting Daddy and she speaks Spanish. Allen wouldn't shake her hand."

When she hears this, Mom looks the way she did when we were at this Indian restaurant and she found out that her curry was made with goat meat. "Hmmm," she says.

Allen tries to make her feel better. "She's nothing, Mom. She's just visiting. And she's an idiot, she barely put a sentence together." I've noticed that Al does this a lot with Mom, tries to take care of her.

That night, I fall asleep imagining Dad's reasons for bringing Paloma home with him. Maybe he's just trying to make Mom jealous. I bet he'll ship Paloma back to Machu Picchu as soon as Mom takes him back. I run through this scenario twelve times in my head, unable to make myself believe it, no matter how hard I try.

KEATIE'S SCHOOL IS HAVING A RECYCLING DRIVE, AND WHICH-ever class brings in the most paper, cans, and whatever else to be recycled wins an ice cream party. She is plundering the house for all things recyclable and keeps interrupting me while I'm trying to choreograph.

"Is this recyclable?" she asks, holding up a milk carton, with milk still in it.

"No," I tell her. "Stick to cans and paper."

She's back again five minutes later, hefting a plastic Stater Brothers bag. "What about these?" she asks, taking out some empty bottles.

"Yes," I tell her, annoyed. But when I look again, I notice that they are vodka bottles. "Where did you get those?"

"I'm not telling."

"Keatie," I say in my most authoritative voice, "tell me."

"Okay, fine. From our big trash can outside. I couldn't find anything else in the house, so I looked in the trash. They were in there."

Weird. My mom isn't a big drinker. . . . At least, I don't think she is.

"Well, stop going through the trash. It's gross."

Keatie goes back upstairs and I can hear her shuffling around, still searching.

another step on the path to sanity

↕

When Thursday rolls around, I am still freaked out about my dad and the Peruvian woman. So much so that I forget that I don't actually answer any of the questions Lisz asks me. When she asks me, "How have you been? What's been going on?" I blurt out, "My dad got back from Peru on Tuesday," without even thinking.

"I didn't know he was in Peru," Lisz says.

Having trapped myself, I decide to give it to her straight for once. What the hell. Things can't get much worse on the Dad front anyway. "Yeah, he joined a hiking club after he moved out and they hiked to Machu Picchu. We saw him last night."

"Oh. So how was it seeing him again?"

"Weird. He brought a woman. Home with him. From

Peru. A Peruvian. He wanted us to meet him for dinner, and when we got there, there was this woman waiting for us at the table. My dad introduces her and says she's Paloma from Peru. And she goes, 'I am Paloma; I am of Peru.' She doesn't speak much English, I guess."

Lisz looks like she's trying to hide a smile. "Does your dad speak Spanish?"

"Yeah. He speaks it all the time for his job."

"That's right," says Lisz, "I forgot." She looks a little embarrassed. I wonder if she ever gets her patients' lives and problems confused. She looks at me expectantly. Probably not.

I finish the story, leaving out the parts about Mom's sad, scared face and Allen's refusal to shake Paloma's hand. Those things seem too personal. Lisz asks a few questions about my feelings toward Paloma ("I don't have any feelings about her: I don't even know her") and then our time is up. I am kind of embarrassed that I didn't have to use the jar, that I've actually discussed part of my life, however tiny it was, with a shrink.

As I wait in the waiting room for Allen to finish his session with Lisz, I do my history homework. Surprisingly, I am able to concentrate for the first time in weeks; for once, what I read actually makes sense. If I didn't know better, I'd think that talking had actually helped somehow. But that's ridiculous. How could the recap of a disaster possibly do anything to clean up the wreckage?

he said, she said

WHEN WE DRIVE HOME, I ASK ALLEN WHAT HE TALKS TO Lisz about.

"None of your business. What do you talk to her about?"

"I talk to her about you, mostly," I say.

He believes me for a split second. "You do?"

I try not to laugh.

"Whatever. You do not. Why do you care what I talk to her about, anyway?"

"Well, do you answer all her questions?" I watch his face, so I can see if he's lying.

"I think so. Why?"

"Do you always tell her the truth?"

"Why wouldn't I?" He makes eye contact with me briefly.

"Because she asks about personal stuff. And what if you don't want to tell her all of it?"

"I guess you just tell her you don't want to talk about it. But so what if you do tell her personal stuff? She's not going to tell anybody anyway. She can't. It's illegal."

"It is? Then why does she always talk about the conversations she's had with you during our sessions?"

He turns up the radio and doesn't respond.

I wonder what would happen if I did tell the whole truth and nothing but the truth.

to the rescue

HALEY AND I HAVE THIS CLASS CALLED ETHICS, AND EVERY Monday the teacher puts up an "ethical dilemma" that the kids in the class have to answer and write about. This week's dilemma:

> A *building is burning down. Two people are alive inside, and only one can be saved. One of the people is your ninety-year-old grandmother, who is immobile and has to use a respirator to help her breathe. The other is a nineteen-year-old man who was recently released from a juvenile detention center. Whom do you save and why?*

Questions like these aren't very interesting to me, and as I try to come up with an answer, one thought repeats in my head: Me. I'd save myself.

shells

Haley's family doesn't cook. Okay, they do, but only once or twice a week, and they almost always make one of the following three meals:

(1) chicken pasta salad.

(2) stuffed shells (my personal favorite).

(3) chicken or vegetable stir-fry, depending on who cooks. Vegetable if Haley's sister Starr is cooking—she'll eat meat, but she won't touch it or cook it; chicken if Haley is cooking. Haley will touch and cook meat for the rest of her family, but she won't eat it, so she always makes a little for herself without chicken. I've asked her why she doesn't just make veggie stuff, and she says it's because she's cooking for her family, not just herself, so she likes to make them what they like. I told

my mom about this and she said, "Haley is an old soul, Mia. A good friend to have."

Sometimes when Haley's brother Max comes home from college and visits, he makes fish sticks, because they're his favorite. No one really eats them but him.

There are seven kids in Haley's family and both of her parents work, so rather than Haley's mom cooking every night, what they usually do is put one of the kids who can drive "in charge of dinner." This means that the person takes Haley's mom's ATM card, gets some money from the machine, and buys food. There's always a huge supply of cold cereal, Easy Cheese, Wheat Thins, and yogurt on hand at Haley's house, but for actual meals, you have to bring in supplies. Sometimes the person in charge of dinner feels ambitious and goes to the grocery store and makes one of the three standard meals, but usually the person buying the takeout will go to one of four restaurants:

(1) Fiesta Time.

(2) SuperSubs.

(3) King Phillip's Spaghetti Barn (where they always get pizza; the spaghetti is pretty gross).

(4) Chopstix (it's a Chinese place, of course).

Before my parents went AWOL, my mom always cooked for us, five days a week, without fail. We'd help her out once in a while, but Mom always planned the meals and just told us what to chop and when to add it. Lately, though, she's made a habit of thawing, warming, or microwaving rather than cooking, and that's only when she doesn't call from work and tell us to get takeout or pizza, or give us directions for how to microwave, thaw, or warm our own meals.

Mom leaves a message on my cell phone during dance practice; I listen to it on the late bus home.

"Would you mind being in charge of dinner tonight, sweetie? I'll be home a little late, and I thought you could just throw together a salad and some spaghetti or something. If you need anything from the store, call Allen and ask him to bring it home when he gets off work. He's got a short shift today, he'll just be there until six. And could you pick up Keatie on your way home from practice? She's at Chewy's. I love you. You're a big help." She makes a kissing sound. "Mmmmmwah. Thanks."

Images of King Phillip's spaghetti and fish sticks flash through my mind. I can see where this is going.

Haley comes over to help me cook. We have all the ingredients we need to make stuffed shells except the shells and the ricotta cheese, which Allen brings home.

He drops a grocery bag onto the counter. "This should be good. You cooking. Do you want me to invite your lover to come over for dinner so that he can see your domestic side?" He must be in a really good mood. He's never encouraged me to hang out with Julian before.

"Shut up."

Haley laughs.

Allen puts his arm around her. "Now that friends of siblings are no longer off limits, what do you say about you and me, Haley? Wanna give it a shot?"

"You remind me too much of my own brothers. Sorry."

"Hey, I understand, but if you ever change your mind, you know where to find me, eh?"

"Checkstand three, right?"

"For now, but I may be promoted to produce soon, so look for me by the radishes if you don't see me there. Well, ladies, I'll leave you to your work," he says as he walks out of the kitchen.

"Typical." I call after him, "You're not even going to offer to help?"

"I brought home the cheese," he yells back.

Haley fills a pot with water and puts it on the stove to boil while I mix herbs, ricotta, and mozzarella cheese in a bowl.

"This feels weird. I know it's normal and I've just been spoiled, having my mom cook all the time. But I still don't like this, you know?" I can say things to Haley that sound selfish and whiny without worrying that she'll think I'm selfish and whiny.

"Moms who cook are an endangered species these days," she says absently.

Keatie walks into the kitchen. "My dad cooks with Paloma," she tells us.

This is news to me. "I can't remember the last time he cooked with Mom. Does your dad ever help your mom cook?" I ask Haley.

"When Mom is in charge of dinner, Dad drives with her to Fiesta Time."

"Close enough."

"I hope so."

"I like cracking eggs," Keatie announces. "Mom showed me how. Can I crack some eggs for dinner?"

"Sure." Haley looks at me and shrugs as if to say "Why not?" "Crack some into that mix of Mia's. It couldn't hurt."

"Cool," says Keatie. "How many can I do?"

"One," I say at the same time Haley says, "Three, maybe?"

"You can do two, and that's it," I tell her.

"All riiiiight!" Keatie gets two eggs out of the refrigerator and enthusiastically cracks them into the bowl.

While we are bobbing for eggshell, the doorbell rings three times in a row. This is Julian's way of signaling that he's coming in and that no one has to bother to answer the door. My heart starts to beat really fast and my fingers can no longer function at the level required to retrieve eggshell particles.

"Hello, domestic goddesses," Julian says as he walks into the kitchen. "What culinary delight are you preparing this evening?"

"Pasta with eggs in it," Keatie tells him.

"Sounds . . . interesting." Julian comes up beside me and whispers, "I need to consult with you about the menu."

"What?"

"Would you please follow me to the dining area?"

Haley rolls her eyes and shoves the two of us out of the kitchen.

Julian leads me to the hallway. "I'm here to see Al, but I wanted to say hi to you. So, um, hi."

"Hi."

At that moment, Allen emerges from the hallway. "Hi," he says. "Well, now we've all said it. Come on, Julio, we've got work to do."

Julian looks embarrassed and I feel stupid. I walk back into the kitchen, where Haley is finishing up with the shells. She looks at me and laughs. "What happened? You look like you got caught passing notes in class."

"It was nothing . . . really."

"You've got a lot of nothing going on lately, huh?" Haley sounds annoyed. She shoves the pan into the oven. "Well, if there's nothing to talk about, let's go catch up on some quality game-show time while the food's cooking."

When the shells are done, we wait for Mom to get home and eat with us, but she calls and says we should eat without her. Keatie leaves a note for her on the table before she goes to bed.

Mommy,

We saved you some dinner. I cracked the eggs. Then I did my homework and beat Allen at ProSoccer twice.

Love,

Your daughter Keatie

Allen adds to the note.

I really beat Keatie. She is lying. And I bought the cheese.

Your son, Allen

Keatie gets mad, writes:

Mom,

I really won. Allen should get in trouble for teasing.

She draws an eye, a heart, and the letter *U* and signs her name. Before Haley leaves, she adds to the note:

Allen really should get in trouble for teasing.
Love,
Haley

Mom still isn't home by the time I go to bed. I add to the note,

Mom,

I love you. I miss your cooking. It would be nice to see you once in a while.

Mia

the kiss

After school Allen is missing; he doesn't have soccer practice, and his car isn't in the parking lot. I run into Julian while I'm looking for Haley.

"Have you seen my brother? Or Haley?"

"No and no. What's going on?"

"I need a ride home, and I can't find anyone."

"You found me."

Since Julian asked me to prom, things have been a little awkward between us. Especially when we're alone together. I think Julian may be worried about what Allen thinks of his asking me to prom. I don't want Julian to think that I think I'm his girlfriend or something just because he asked me. I can't just ask him for a ride home, like I would've before;

he might think I expect him to drive me all over just because he asked me.

"Hello?" Julian says, knocking gently on my head.

I've been standing there thinking, staring into space without realizing it.

"Yeah, um, I'm looking for a ride home."

"Is my car not good enough for you? What's the deal?"

"I didn't realize you had offered me a ride."

"Are you crazy? Since when do I need to issue a formal invitation to give you a ride home? Come on."

Great. Now I've managed to make a huge deal out of nothing, out of a ride home.

Julian bows in front of me. "Mimoo. Meezer-Mia, my lady. I want to give you a ride. Home, I mean." He grabs my hand, kisses it, and holds it for a moment while we walk to the car. My heart is beating so fast it feels like it's going to launch out of my chest. He opens the door for me, but he always does that.

"I'm a total dork," I tell him as he starts the car. Why do I say things like that? Why don't I just put up a billboard that says, JULIAN, MIA'S AN IDIOT, THERE'S A REASON YOU DIDN'T LIKE HER BEFORE, AND IT HASN'T REALLY CHANGED.

"I know you're a dork." He raises his eyebrows. "And I like it."

"You would, you pervert."

"You haven't seen perverted yet, baby." He puts his hand on my knee and makes a half suggestive, half comical face.

I love being with him; I love the way things are still the same, but different, too. I love the possibilities in what he says now that were never there before. It's hard to rein myself in, though, and not start talking to him about how I just know we're going to fall madly in love and get married and have babies and grow old together. I am ready to be absolutely crazy obsessed in love with Julian. I mean, I am already, right? I wish I knew what Julian thought. How much does he really like me? I could fixate on this line of thought for hours, but it never gets me anywhere.

When we get to my house, there are no cars in the driveway.

"Look. I'm a total latchkey kid now." I give him a pathetic look, thrusting my lower lip out. My mom used to work half days at the office. She was almost always home when we got home from school. She seems to have started working full-time without ever telling us.

"Welcome to the club, you ex–spoiled brat."

"Sorry." I forget that Julian's been going home to an empty house for years. Smart, Mia, real smart.

"I'm joking," he tells me.

"Right. Does Keatie's team have practice tonight?"

"Yeah, at six. I hope Al shows. He missed a practice last week."

"Really? That's not like him. Playing soccer and telling people what to do are two of his favorite things."

"He's developed some new hobbies lately."

I remember the phone calls from school, the way his car is never in the parking lot, the mysterious empty bottles. "Like what?"

"I don't know." Julian shrugs; he sounds awkward, unsure. "Maybe I should stay and wait with you. So I can remind Al about practice when he gets back."

I look at him like he's nuts. "Sure. Come on in." I'm actually relieved that Julian doesn't say anything about Allen. It's probably better that I don't know what's going on.

Julian has a thing for science. He likes watching the Discovery Channel. During a show about African ecosystems, he kisses me for the first time. And then the second, and then the third, and then I lose count.

While Julian is kissing me, I think about how I love his hair and the way it feels to run my fingers through it. I think about his shoulders, how much wider they are than mine, the way the muscles in them tighten when I kiss his neck. After I sort of get used to the idea of his kissing me, of Julian Paynter's actually liking me enough to kiss me, I think about the other girls I know he's kissed—there are three. Two of them I liked okay; one of them I don't know, a random girl he met at the beach two summers ago. I remember how when I kissed Miguel in Mexico, I was disappointed that it felt the same as kissing anybody else, not different because he was from another country. I think about my parents: my dad and Paloma, my mom in the bed she sleeps in alone. And then I think about Julian some more, how much I like looking at his legs when he wears those dumb long soccer socks, how I'd never quite been able to imagine kissing him, but how I've always known that it would feel like flying and coming home at the same time.

Julian leaves at five-thirty and Al still hasn't come home. When I say goodbye to Julian at the door, his face looks flushed, like he's just run a few miles, and I wonder if mine looks that way, too. After he's gone I look at myself in the mirror, expecting to find myself glowing or transformed somehow, but I look the way I always do, except most of my makeup has been kissed off. I think again about my parents, how they used to kiss in front of us, how we always thought it was so disgusting.

I decide to ask Julian to drive me home more often. Maybe I'll put off getting my driver's license until he goes away to college.

cats and bags

I ARRIVE HOME FROM A LATE DANCE PRACTICE AND AM surprised to find my mom and Julian's mom sitting outside drinking Diet Cokes and talking. When they see me, they stop.

"Hey. What's going on?" I ask. "Is everything okay?"

They look at each other and smile like there's some kind of secret between them.

"Everything's fine, Mia. I decided that I was working too much, so I came home early, and Hope and I were just chatting."

"Oh. Hi, Hope." So Mom's noticed; she's returning to her home planet. Maybe she's going to start acting like my mom again.

"Hello."

She and my mom look at each other again and smile.

"What?" I demand. "Why are you guys acting so weird?"

My mom and Hope have been hanging out more since my dad moved out. They went to a cooking class together once, and last week Mom invited Hope to the opening night of some opera at the Orange County Performing Arts Center.

"We were just talking, Mia. You know, girl talk," my mom says.

"Yeah, just some old ladies having a little girl talk," Hope adds.

Allen pulls into the driveway; Keatie waves at us frantically from the passenger seat and hops out of the car almost before it has stopped moving.

"Were you talking about me?" I ask.

They both laugh.

"No. Not at all," says Hope.

I look at them suspiciously, trying to figure out what's going on.

"M-o-o-o-o-m!" Keatie shrieks as she runs up the porch steps. She throws her arms around my mother as if she hasn't seen her in years.

"Someone has been playing soccer and sweating up a storm," Mom says as she hugs Keatie.

"We scrimmaged and I scored three times," Keatie reports. She notices Julian's mother. "Hey, Hope. Guess what? I've seen Mia kissing Julian with her eyes closed."

"What?" I yelp.

Allen hears this as he walks up the steps, and groans. "That is something I do not need to hear."

"I need to have a serious talk with you," Mom says to Allen, as if she hasn't even registered Keatie's outburst.

Hope stands up. "That's my cue to leave."

"I'm starving," Keatie announces, and goes inside.

"Me too," I say, following Keatie into the house.

As I walk in, I hear my mom saying something to Allen about calls from the school and unexcused absences.

"You know you have to graduate from high school in order to go to college," she tells him as I shut the door to my room.

Relieved that my mother seems to have resumed the job of worrying about what's going on in our family, I fall asleep until dinner. Maybe things can go back to normal now. Maybe she'll superglue the pieces of our family back together, so that even if we were in a head-on collision, no one would fall out of place.

two birds

"DO YOU WANT TO GO TO THE BAGEL PLACE FOR LUNCH today?" Julian asks on the way to school. He and Allen need to discuss strategy for Keatie's game on Saturday—the biggest one of the season, according to them—so they're carpooling to maximize their planning time. They're in the front seats of Allen's bus; I'm in the back.

"Sure," Allen and I say at the same time.

"Oops. Sorry," I say, "I thought you were talking to me."

"I was. . . . I mean, I was talking to both of you."

"Actually, I don't have time to go; I need to do some homework during lunch. So you guys should go without me," Allen says.

Things have gotten a bit uncomfortable among the three of us. I think it's the most awkward for Allen, though. The other day, Allen called Julian after he got off work, wanting to hang out, but I was already at Julian's. Sometimes when Julian comes over to see Allen, he'll call me beforehand to let me know. I am never sure what I'm supposed to do when he does that—put on more makeup, leave the house . . . it gets weird.

Allen gives me the keys when I get out of the car. "You can drive Julian to lunch, you know, to practice for your driving test, but if you do anything to my car, you're dead."

"Thanks. I promise I'll be careful."

"Al, that's cool of you," Julian tells him. "Maybe not so smart, though. Have you seen Meezer drive?"

On the way to lunch, I almost rear-end three cars.

"It's back to empty parking lots for you," Julian says.

"I was just nervous because I haven't practiced much in Al's car. I'm not really that bad."

Julian looks skeptical.

We walk into the bagel store and get in line. Kiki Nordgren is a few people ahead of us.

"Hey, Julian." She makes the "hey" sound like it has two syllables. She ignores me.

Julian nods at her. "Hi, Kiwi," he says loudly. He whispers in my ear, "She hates that, but she'll act like she didn't notice."

And that, ladies and gentlemen, is why he is my favorite boy on the planet.

Kiki smiles at him and turns back to her friends.

When we get to the cash register, Julian pays for my bagel sandwich, like we're on a date. He tells me about his mom and her boyfriend while we eat.

"He's lame. I mean, he doesn't *do* anything. He manages the freaking appliance department at Sears; that's it. My mom worked her ass off to go to college after my dad left, so that she could get an education, you know, a good job, and that guy just hangs out at Sears all day."

"That sucks. But she's not stupid. She must see something in him."

"I think she's just lonely. . . . Anyway, he's at our house all the time. He spent the night last Friday. She doesn't think I know, but I heard him leave in the morning."

"Gross. Maybe we can set him up with Paloma, kill two birds with one stone."

"I wish," he says. "Speaking of setting people up, we need to find Allen a date for prom. He still hasn't asked anyone; he says it's a waste of money and he doesn't want to go."

"I'll start looking for prospects," I tell him.

While I drive back to school, Julian turns on a country radio station and tries to get me to sing a duet with him.

"Neither of us even knows this song," I say. "Besides, I have to concentrate. You're distracting me."

"Part of learning to drive is learning to deal effectively with distractions," he says.

Later on, I think about what Julian said: maybe part of learning to live is learning to deal effectively with distractions. But how do you tell the difference between a distraction and something you really should pay attention to?

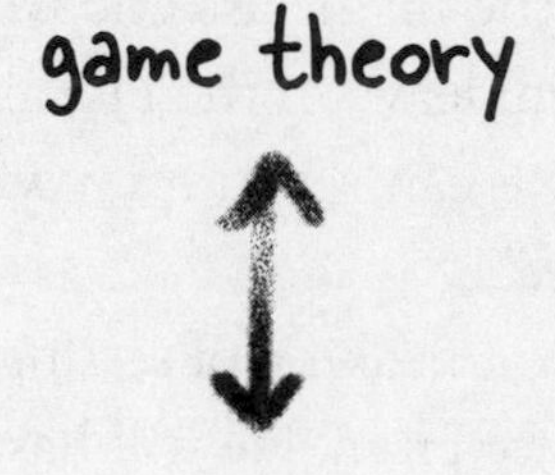

JULIAN'S AT MY HOUSE PLAYING SOME GAME WHERE HE RIPS the heads off trolls and dragons. I am pretending to do my homework, the way I did before he asked me to prom, before he kissed me. It's confusing. I don't know how I'm supposed to act. It'd be great if I could just make out with him all the time, I guess, but I don't know what he wants. I don't know how much different the before and after are supposed to look when it comes to us. Sometimes I want to ask him, just so I don't have to wonder and feel so awkward all the time. But I don't want him to think I'm crazy.

"Any luck finding Al a prom date?" Julian asks me.

"Why don't we try to get him to take Haley?" I suggest. "Mike Hickenlooper wants to ask her."

"Mike Hickenlooper? Really? I thought he was with Kiera Garcia."

"Nope. She dumped him. Did you see that?" He motions to the game. "His spinal cord came out with his head, that doesn't always happen."

"Gross. So is he going to ask Haley?"

"Who knows?"

"What if he gets back together with Kiera, then what happens to Haley? She'll end up at the prom with a guy who wants to be with someone else."

"This conversation is starting to sound too much like a female conspiracy. And I just got fried by a dragon. Let's just forget about prom for a while; I'm sorry I brought it up. It'll all work out somehow."

communication breakdown

I'M TALKING TO JULIAN ON THE PHONE AND THE OTHER LINE rings. Haley's number flashes on the caller ID screen.

"Haley's calling," I tell him.

"Oh, do you need to go, then?"

"Nah, I'll call her later."

A few minutes later, our conversation is interrupted again, this time by Allen. He has picked up the extension in his room. "Hey, Meezer, how much longer are you gonna be on this thing? I need to call Julio and I can't find my cell phone."

"Um, well . . . Julian's on the phone right now. Do you want to talk to him and just let me know when you're done?"

"Julio? You there?"

"Yeah," Julian answers.

"Oh. Uh . . . never mind, man. I'll talk to you later."

Allen's voice sounds strange. All of a sudden I feel really dumb. Like I'm eleven years old again, bugging Julian and Allen to let me play video games with them, just so I can be around Julian.

"Yeah, I'll give you a call in a few," Julian says.

Allen hangs up. We sit there in silence for a few seconds.

"Hey, listen, Julian, I've got homework to do, so I'd better go." I don't really have much homework at all, but I feel weird about talking to Julian now.

"Yeah, and I need to talk to Al, so . . ."

"See ya."

"Bye."

I click the phone off.

I don't remember to call Haley back until late that night when I check my cell phone messages and there are three from her.

"Mia, I really need to talk to you. Call me."

"Mimoo, it's me again. Call me, call me, call me!"

"Meems, I'm going to bed now. I guess we'll talk tomorrow."

When I see her at school, I ask her what she needed to talk to me about.

"Mike Hickenlooper called me and asked me for our math assignment and he isn't even in my class. He's pretty cute, don't you think?"

"Yeah. But isn't he dating Kiera Garcia?"

"Maybe. I don't keep up on stuff like that. . . . So you don't think . . ." Her voice trails off.

“Things have been weird with me and Allen and Julian lately,” I tell her.

Haley listens to my story, but she seems kind of distracted. She’s usually much more focused when we talk. The bell rings.

“Argh. Class.” Haley groans.

“I know. Doesn’t it feel like just yesterday that we had the exact same classes at the exact same time?” I joke. “I feel like we never hang out anymore. Are you busy today after school?”

“Nope.”

“Do you want to do something? Maybe play a little tennis?” I like playing tennis with Haley. Even though she’s a superstar player, she doesn’t mind how bad I am. She just plays along. Most people, especially Allen and my dad, don’t deal as well with mediocrity. Allen has freaked out on me a few times when I’ve tried to play soccer, and my dad used to get really annoyed with Allen when he couldn’t understand his math homework.

“Sure. Let’s just meet at my car after school.”

“You got it. See you there.” I make a graceless tennis-racket-swinging motion as I walk away.

the backup plan

"WOULD YOU GO TO THE PROM WITH AL IF HE ASKED YOU?" I ask Haley, looking at the strings on my racket and sort of clawing them with my fingers. I've seen tennis players on TV do this, and I'm trying to look like I don't really care what Haley says, so I continue to feel the strings while I wait for her answer.

"Why are you asking? And what are you doing with your racket?"

Haley and I took tennis lessons together in elementary school. She was great; I was okay. It didn't bother me because she was my best friend, and when she whipped someone's ass, I felt like I'd had some part in it. It's hard to be jealous of Haley. She's too nice. My mother says she's very grounded. Except when it comes to boys. She gets pretty jumpy around guys she likes, and she's fairly oblivious when someone she isn't interested in likes her.

Once, this nerdy kid, Ricky Friedman, kept asking her to hang out, and she kept saying okay because she felt bad for him. She didn't realize that he thought they were dating, so she totally freaked out when he tried to kiss her one night. They were at the movies when he tried it, and she got up, told him she needed to use the bathroom, left the theater, and called her mom from a Wendy's down the street. We call that night "The Ricky Friedman Debacle," and whenever anyone Haley isn't into asks her out, she always says no, even if they just want to be friends. "I can't handle another Ricky Friedman Debacle," she says.

"I'm checking to make sure my strings are okay," I tell her now. "And I'm asking because Allen has no one to go with and Julian really wants Allen to go with us. He could end up going with someone awful and then the whole night would suck."

"I don't know, Meems. I can't—"

"He's no Ricky Friedman, Haley. C'mon. I mean, maybe he already has someone in mind to ask, but if he doesn't, would you go with him? Are you really into Mike Hickenlooper?"

"What? I thought you said he was with Kiera Garcia."

"So you aren't into him?" I feel a little guilty about not telling Haley what Julian told me about Mike's having a crush on her, but if she doesn't even like him, it's not a big deal, right? Plus Haley will have more fun with us than with someone she barely knows.

"I guess not. Why?"

"No reason. Would you go with Al if he asked you?"

"Sure. I guess. Can we play now?"

"Yeah. Of course."

I know it sounds crazy, but it feels so nice to feel like you are in control of something, however small it is. The rest of my life has gone haywire, but I will have a perfect prom night.

"Great. Let me call Julian and tell him." I put down the racket, race over to my backpack, and get out my phone.

"What? Why are you calling Julian?"

I signal for her to be quiet—the phone is ringing. Julian doesn't answer, so I leave a message.

When I hang up, Haley is staring at me. She looks a little sad, a little pissed off. "You know what, Meems? I'm tired. Let's just go home."

"Are you sure? Is everything okay?"

"Yeah, everything's fine. Let's just go."

I wonder what's going on with Haley. She's been acting weird lately.

At home that night, I still can't shake the way I feel about not telling her about Mike Hickenlooper. It's one thing not telling her about what's going on with me, but it's different to not tell her things about her. I think of calling her and telling her, but I decide against it. She'll understand, right? She always does.

another thursday visit, or the only thing we have to fear . . .

I NOTICE DURING THIS VISIT TO LISZ'S OFFICE THAT HER COUCH is purple, not black. I had assumed, because the color was so dark, that it was black. Wrongo Pongo, it's purple. A very deep plum. I realize this because I have been staring at the couch for three solid minutes without actually speaking.

I grab the jar, take out a piece of paper: *your greatest fear*.

"It says 'your greatest fear.' "

I think about the potter's wheel, unused, in our garage, the diploma hanging on the wall of my father's office, the white line around the ring finger of my mother's left hand.

"My greatest fear is being caught in a fire, or maybe heights."

"What about those two things, specifically, makes you

afraid?" Lisz asks as she leans forward, putting her elbows on her knees, propping her head up with her hands.

I stare at her nails, a muted tangerine color.

"I guess I hate pain—and being burned would be really painful. I saw this episode of *ER* where this kid was burned and they had to, like, peel his burned skin off."

I expect her to look grossed out, but she acts as if she hears this every day.

"And I hate heights because I hate the idea of falling. And splatting on the ground."

"I see," she says. "So you've expressed a great fear of physical pain. . . ."

She asks me questions about pain: whether I had any experiences as a child where I suffered severe physical pain, whether I've been threatened with physical pain as some sort of punishment for disobedience, things like that. I consider lying, making up a story about my dad beating me with a belt for not cleaning my room, but I decide against it. I don't want to get my parents turned in to the police or anything.

"Mia, you concentrate a lot on the exterior, on the physical, in our visits. What about the interior, the mental or emotional? Do you fear that kind of pain as well?"

What kind of a question is that? Are there people out there who relish the idea of emotional anguish?

Lisz looks at me expectantly.

"I guess."

She acts as if I have just revealed a secret that has the potential to alter the study of psychiatry as we know it.

"Okay, Mia." She speaks cautiously, like she's the Crocodile Hunter and I am the wild animal she's trying to trap. "Tell me a little more about that."

I don't respond. She's given herself away; I know that she's trying to trick me into saying something I don't want to say.

"Why don't you name things you think people are afraid of, and I'll tell you if those things scare me or not," I suggest.

"I don't think that's the most effective way to go about this. Do you think there might be a better way of discussing this issue?"

"Like what?" I ask.

"Well, if I try to guess what's going on inside you—what it is that you fear—we could sit here for hours and never get anywhere. I do have some ideas about how certain things have affected you and how you've chosen to react to them, but it's important that you recognize these things for yourself."

"Oh. But if you're a professional, don't you think you'd be better at knowing what bugs me or what makes me crazy than I would?"

"Mia. First of all, you aren't crazy. You aren't here because you are crazy or because anyone thinks you are going crazy. Second, you are here to learn about yourself by thinking and talking about your experiences, how you've responded to them and why you've responded to them the way you have, not for me to tell you who you are and why. I'm not a psychic; I'm a psychiatrist."

"Right. Well, can I pick a different paper, then?"

After vetoing several topics, I settle on *your best friend.* I talk about Haley and the time I tried to perm her hair when we were in fourth grade, how I ended up frying it so badly that she had to cut all her hair off, and how she looked a lot like a young Matt Damon with her hair so short.

Lisz asks me if our relationship has changed since my parents began having problems.

"No," I lie, "things are the same as always." The same as always except that now we hardly see each other, act like strangers when we do, don't really talk, and she seems kinda pissed at me when we do talk. Yep, things are great. Totally normal. I've just been hiding the fact that this boy who she might actually like (which never happens) might actually like her. Something I would probably never forgive her for if she did it to me. Only, Haley would never in a million years do anything like that to me. But yeah, we're best friends and everything is fine. I just suck, that's all.

"How does it make you feel to know that your relationship with Haley hasn't changed, even though so many other things in your life have?"

"Good," I tell her, "like there's at least one thing I can count on, like not everything had to change or get all messed up because of the divorce." It seems like that's what she was going for. Sometimes it's easy to read Lisz; sometimes it's more difficult, depending on her questions. Sometimes I understand what she's trying to get me to see, what she wants me to say, and it makes sense. She wants me to see what I have, what I can do with it. She wants me to see what's changed and figure out how to deal with it.

While I wait for Allen to finish his session with Lisz, I call Haley. Her phone goes straight to voice mail: "Hi, you've reached Haley's cell phone. I try not to use this thing very much because it probably causes brain cancer, and I try to live as noncarcinogenic a life as possible. So leave a message and I'll call you back from a landline."

"Hi, it's me." I think about telling Haley about Mike right now, but I can't. "Where are you? I miss you. I feel like a jerk about the other day. I'm sorry for being such an idiot lately. Call me . . . if you can find it in your heart to forgive me."

adaptation

JULIAN WILL WAX POETIC ON OCCASION, USUALLY WHEN HE ponders the mysteries unfolded to him in his advanced biology class.

"We're losing pieces of ourselves, Meezer. It's the way life works."

"What?" I ask, breathless. He likes to think about this stuff when we're kissing, I think; he has this tendency to interrupt really great make-outs with his musings on science.

"In evolution, it takes a long time, you know, for things to be lost, to disappear. Like how we're going to lose our pinky toes eventually. And we've already lost tons of teeth."

"We're not going to have pinky toes anymore?"

"Maybe not."

"But they're my favorite toes. Why can't we lose the freaky second toe?"

He shrugs and looks like he's ready to kiss me again.

But I'm already distracted. "It's weird how some people's second toes are longer than their big toes."

"And the crazy thing is, that stuff doesn't come back," he says. "Once you lose it, it's gone."

I don't say anything.

"And that's just one example of how biology, which is life, essentially, is about losing things. Really it's about change, I guess, but for humans, for people who live in the modern world, most of our adaptations have to do with losing things, with how we don't need to be as strong anymore."

I look at him, put my hands on his cheeks, kiss his eyelids, then the three freckles on his forehead.

"I hope we never adapt out of freckles," I say, and I feel like crying.

late blooms

MOST GIRLS DEVELOP BREASTS IN JUNIOR HIGH SCHOOL. I didn't get boobs until I was almost fifteen. I guess that wouldn't have been that bad except for the fact that, having skipped a grade, I was already a year behind everyone else. I was a sophomore in high school by the time I really needed a bra, and I still can't even fill out a B-cup.

Kiki Nordgren has had a rack since she was twelve.

This all brings me to the realization I had today: Julian has never tried to feel me up. I wonder if he is gay. Or if he hates my boobs.

It's 6:20 a.m. I am supposed to be at dance practice in ten minutes, but Allen is not awake and ready to take me like he's supposed to be. I knock on his door. No response. I open the door and walk quietly over to his bed, which doesn't make sense since I am about to wake him up. He's dead asleep.

"Al, wake up." I nudge his shoulder.

He doesn't respond.

I say it again, louder, and shake him harder.

"Ow," he croaks. "What? No. Too early." He rolls over so his back is facing me.

I shake him again. "You said you'd take me to practice this morning. I can't be late."

"Can't, Mimoo. Too tired. Must have the flu or something," he mumbles, turning over in the bed so that he faces me.

When he does this, his breath hits me, and I know he doesn't just have the flu, if he is really even sick at all.

"Have you been *drinking*?" I ask.

"Too tired. Need to sleep. Ask Julian to take you."

"Is he hungover, too?"

He opens his eyes and shields them with his arm. "Are you crazy? Julian? Come on. Please . . . turn that light off." He rolls back over and pulls his sheet over his head.

I call Julian.

"Hey, sorry to call so early. Can you take me to dance practice? Al can't, and I don't want to have to explain why to my parents."

"Huh?"

"I can't talk about it right now. Can you take me or not?"

"Easy, tiger. Yeah, I'll take you. Can you walk over here while I'm getting dressed?"

"Sure."

I walk to Julian's, knock on his front door, walk into the house, and wait in the living room. He comes out with his toothbrush in his mouth. He points to it and to his watch, tries to say something. I guess he is trying to tell me that we'll leave as soon as he finishes brushing his teeth.

He disappears again. I hear him running the water in the bathroom and spitting. He reemerges, keys in hand.

"So what happened with Al?" he asks as we get into his car.

"He's hungover. Or maybe he's still drunk. I don't know. Either way, he's been drinking. Do you know anything about this?"

"Last night after the game some guys decided to go out, but usually that just means pizza. Are you sure he was drinking? Not just tired?"

"I think I know the difference between the smells of alcohol and morning breath. He's been drinking."

"Wow. Today's Tuesday. I mean, it's not even a weekend."

"Yeah." I think about this for a moment. "Wait, are you saying that if it was a weekend, this would be normal?"

"Not exactly," he says, hedging, "but it's not like your brother's partying is anything new, right?"

"It's not?" I remember the canteen in his backpack, the calls from school, the way he's always disappearing from home, driving off by himself.

"Oh. Right. Maybe it is. I'll ask him what happened."

"Thanks." But I don't want Julian to just ask him what happened. I want him to fix it, or I want somebody to fix it, or erase it. I don't know how to talk about real problems, much less how to resolve them, but I wish someone did.

Neither of us can find anything else to say, so we listen to a band I've never heard of sing a song about French fries and Eskimos.

When we get to the school, he kisses me quickly on the lips and says, in an effeminate voice, "You dance your little heart out, you hear me? You little dancing Eskimo, you."

I laugh before I can stop myself, grab my bag from the backseat, and get out of the car. "Will you please try to get Al up and to school? He's already in trouble for missing so much."

"Aye, aye, Captain."

near-deaf experience

↕

BEFORE JULIAN MOVED IN, MOST OF THE KIDS ON THE STREET were lots older than Allen and I, so we hung out with each other a lot. We were best friends because Allen didn't know yet that it wasn't cool to hang out with your younger sister more than anyone else.

Once, we were playing with the hose in the backyard and a bee flew into Allen's ear. I ran inside to tell my mom, who ran outside, saw Allen holding his ear, and then ran back inside to call 911. While Mom panicked, I shoved the hose in Allen's ear, turned the water on full blast, and flushed the bee out. By the time she got through and had explained the situation to an annoyed operator, Allen and I were already back to spraying each other with the hose, and Allen was doing his best to put the hose in my ear to "see if there are any bees in there."

Later, Mom kept talking about how if the bee had stung Allen's eardrum, he could have gone deaf in one ear. I thought I had saved his life, the words *deaf* and *death* sounded so alike to me. Back then, it was that easy to rescue somebody, to make things right.

just asking

ALLEN AND I ARE DRIVING TO LISZ'S, TEN MINUTES LATE because we had to push-start his car. "Have you decided who you're going to take to prom yet?"

"Prom? Meeze, are you kidding?"

"C'mon, you're supposed to go with me and Julian."

"Well, then I guess I do know who I'm taking to prom—you and Julian."

"You know what I mean."

"Right. Okay. I do not have a date to prom, nor do I have any desire to find one."

"Well, I was thinking you could take Haley to prom. She's hot, and you're taller than she is."

"She is somewhat hot, and I am slightly taller than she is."

"So what's the problem?"

"Okay, Mimoo, tell you what, do me a favor. Next time you see Haley, ask her if she'll go to prom with me."

"What?"

"Just ask her if she wants to go with me."

"You can't be serious. You want me to ask her for you? Are you crazy?"

"What's the big deal? You see her more than I do. It'd be weird for me to call her, because I never call her unless it's to ask her to send you home."

"I am not. Going to ask. Haley. To go. To prom. With you."

"Fine. Well, will you at least tell her to call me?"

"Why is this such a big deal? Why are you being such a wuss?"

"Because you're the one who wants me to ask her, so why don't you just do it for me?"

"Whatever."

"I'll think about asking her, okay?"

We are silent for a while. I watch cars pass and try to think about prom dresses, but I still feel uneasy.

I get tired of the tension and blurt out, "You never told me what happened the other morning. When you didn't wake up on time. You were drunk, right? Or hungover?" I keep looking out the window as I say this; I'm afraid to look at Allen's face.

He sighs. "Look, it's no big deal. Don't worry about it."

"Julian said that you—" I begin, turning away from the window to look at him, but he interrupts.

"So you and Julian sit around talking about me now?" His

face is white; he stares straight ahead, gripping the wheel like he's trying to strangle it.

"Forget it."

"No, really." He looks over at me briefly, his face pained. "I am interested to know what my best friend and my little sister have been saying about me. Julian can't come over without you hanging all over him, and I can't just show up at his house anymore, because who knows if you'll be there or not."

"C'mon. That's not how things are."

"Right."

Silence again. We don't speak until we pull into the parking lot of Lisz's office building.

"Do you talk to Lisz about it?" I ask.

"Jeez, Mia. About *what*?"

"Drinking."

"Do *you* talk to Lisz about your shit? The way you go around acting like there's nothing weird going on in our house? You think that by keeping your mouth shut and not saying anything and pretending that the most important things in the world are Julian and your stupid prom you can erase the fact that Dad walked out on us and Mom acts like she can't stand to be around us anymore?"

I hop down from the car without saying anything and rush into the office. I realize as I walk through the glass doors that I forgot to close the car door.

another thursday

THE PAPER IN MY HAND READS: *THE MOST INTERESTING THING about you!*

"There isn't one!" I want to say. But I don't.

I've tried to figure out ways to tell Lisz about myself, to see what she has to say, without telling her it's me. You know, like one of those "I have this friend who . . ." stories, but everyone always knows who those are really about. I've also considered telling her a really awful story about "a friend" and seeing how she reacts, whether she thinks I'm talking about myself.

"Do you ever get bored?" I ask. I like to surprise her.

"Bored? No. Why?"

"It just seems like everyone probably has the same kinds of problems. So I just thought that maybe you got tired of hearing about them all the time."

"What kind of problems do you assume everyone would have?"

"Things like divorce, depression, drug addiction . . . I don't know. It seems like everyone has different problems maybe, but they all come out of the same basic things."

"That's very insightful. What do you think is at the root of most problems, then, Mia?"

"I think people are scared."

"What do you think they are scared of?"

"Of not being good enough, of not being liked or loved or understood."

Lisz picks up a pen and writes something in her notebook. I look at her and then at the notebook to make sure she knows I know what she's doing.

"Do you have those fears, too?"

"Sure. I mean, everyone does."

"Mia, that's an incredible insight. Knowing things like that, understanding what motivates us to turn to unhealthy habits and ways of coping, should really help you to deal with the conflicts that arise in your life." She seems excited.

I wonder why she's acting like I just told her my deepest, darkest secrets. I need to proceed with caution. "Okay."

"Do you think your parents' separation has influenced the way you view yourself and the way others see you?"

"I don't know. But I'm not on drugs or anything and I'm not depressed, either, so probably not." I know I'm lying, but come on, do I really have to spell everything out? Say it out loud in all its embarrassing glory? The thought of digging everything out makes me tired and sad. I think about what Allen said to me about ignoring things, trying to erase them.

"I don't want to push too hard here, Mia, but I think there is something going on. You seem very defensive and set on revealing as little about yourself as possible. That tells me that you must be afraid of something. Something besides dying in a fire. I think there's something going on inside you that you are not ready or willing to deal with."

I don't say anything. I wonder if I'm hiding more than I know; I wonder if I know things I don't think I do.

I go through hypotheticals in my head. What if I did tell her everything I was really afraid of, everything I saw happening—Allen's drinking, Keatie's loneliness, Mom's working and never being home anymore, Dad's starting some new perfect life with a Peruvian slut. What's the worst that could happen?

I could tell her everything and find out that it changes nothing. That there is no way to turn back, to undo, to erase. That there is no way out.

That might be my greatest fear.

knott's scary farm

IT WAS DAD'S IDEA TO TAKE US ALL TO KNOTT'S BERRY FARM with Paloma. At least, that's what Keatie said. Allen and I protest. "You want us to spend an *entire* Sunday with Dad and *that lady*?" he shouts. Allen hardly ever raises his voice at Keatie.

"Dad says we can get funnel cake and go on Montezooma's Revenge as many times as we want!" Keatie acts as if this would be a good enough reason to undergo electroshock therapy, much less spend time with Dad and the Slut.

We all end up going.

Knott's Berry Farm is an amusement park that's set up to seem like some kind of western ghost town–farm. There are a few roller coasters, some other rides, and a section that's mostly for kids called Camp Snoopy.

Before we've driven three minutes in the car, Keatie announces, "I'm not going to ride a single ride at Camp Snoopy. It's for babies."

"What about the airplanes? You love those. You like being the Red Baron," I remind her.

"Nope. Not anymore. I only like the big rides, huh, Allen?"

"Sure thing," he says listlessly. Since the morning I found him hungover, I've noticed that Allen seems much more moody than he was before. I think he drinks more often than I want to know.

Sometimes he's almost giddy, deliriously happy, like how he was a week or so ago when I found him, Julian, and Keatie watching tapes of a championship soccer game Allen played in a few years back. Other times he is sullen and angry, like the other day when he couldn't find Julian and he called me up looking for him. I wasn't even with Julian, but Allen still said, "Ease up on him, Mia. You're going to scare him off."

We let the subject of Camp Snoopy drop and ride to the amusement park in relative silence, except for the Peruvian flute music playing on the stereo and Keatie's occasional comments about how many roller coasters she's going to ride and how she isn't going to throw up even once.

Once we get to Knott's, it doesn't take me long to realize that we're in for an interesting time. Keatie tries to hold Dad's hand whenever he and Paloma start to walk off by themselves. Allen must notice this, too, because pretty soon he's trying to hold Keatie's hand all the time and usually attempting to lead her in the opposite direction, away from Dad and Paloma.

When everyone manages to agree on which ride to go on next, Paloma usually refuses to ride. "Ay, no. *¡Dios mio!*"

So the four of us ride together, yelling and putting our hands in the air to convince Keatie that we're having fun.

About the eighth time my dad speaks to Paloma in Spanish to "translate" what we are saying (Paloma always laughs whenever Dad says anything—something we never do), Keatie gets upset.

"Why do you always talk to her and not us?" she shouts. She sits down on a bench and puts her thumb in her mouth. Dad and Allen speak at the same time: "Keatie, get your thumb out of your mouth."

Keatie reluctantly removes her thumb and wipes it on her jeans.

"Which ride do you want to go on next?" Dad asks, annoyed.

"None," says Keatie.

"What?"

"I don't want to go on any more rides. I want to go home."

"Are you sure?" Dad, Allen, and I ask at the same time.

"Yes," whimpers Keatie.

So we leave.

In the car, on the drive home, Keatie leans forward from the middle of the backseat and turns off the Peruvian flute music. We drive in silence the rest of the way home.

thumbsuckers

KEATIE IS WATCHING HOME MOVIES AGAIN, BUT THIS TIME SHE watches the tape that shows Mom when she was pregnant with her.

Dad pans the camera down Mom's body and zooms in and out when he gets to her belly. "Wow," he says, "three months to go and you already look like you're going to pop any minute."

The camera pans up to show Mom rolling her eyes. "Thanks, Russ. Thanks a lot. That's just what I need to hear."

The camera focuses on the door, and I walk in sucking my thumb. I forgot that when my mom told us she was pregnant, I started sucking my thumb again.

"Thumb out of mouth, Meems, or we'll sing the song," Dad says from behind the camera.

I also forgot that my father's way of trying to get me to stop was to sing a song about a girl named Mia who sucked her thumb so much that her lips fell off.

"Hey," he says as he pans the camera between Mom and me, "Mama . . . Mia . . . Mama . . . Mia . . ."

I take my thumb out of my mouth. "Can't you sing the thumbsucking song instead of that?" I ask him. I also forgot how much I hated the Mama Mia thing. . . . I start to miss it while watching the video. Not really the Mama Mia chant, I guess, but the way we used to do things, the way there were things I could count on, even if they bugged me.

"I want the baby to stay inside of Mommy," I say, and put my thumb back in my mouth.

Keatie stops the tape and looks at me.

"I was six," I tell her. "I'm glad you came out."

Keatie puts her thumb in her mouth, picks up the remote with her free hand, and turns off the video.

treading water

IT'S 10:39 P.M. I OPEN MY HISTORY BOOK. I'M SUPPOSED TO read two chapters by tomorrow and write a list of questions about the end-of-chapter questions. Mr. Bingler is determined to get us to "question what the textbook wants us to believe about America," so instead of answering the damn questions at the end of the chapter, we have to come up with new ones.

The phone rings.

It's Haley. "Let's sneak into the Olympus Lakes pool."

"Can't. History homework."

"I already did it. I'll tell you what's in the chapters on the way over and we can do your questions on the way back."

Yeah, it's cheating; yeah, Haley's a straight-A student with a perfect academic record; and yeah, we've done this a million times over the years. Sometimes I read and report, sometimes Haley does.

Her justification: "It's ethical because we're really just supposed to learn the material; the way we learn it doesn't matter, as long as we learn it."

"Okay. Just us, or should I invite Al and Julian?"

"Just us. It's been a while."

Haley flashes her brights, our signal. My parents'—I guess my mom's now—bedroom faces the backyard, and my bedroom window is visible from the driveway, so when we were younger, Haley used to shine a flashlight in my window to signal that she was there. That was before we all had cell phones, back when my parents would have cared that I was leaving the house at night without their permission. I like that Haley still does it the old way, that to her it's still natural to use our signal, that she's even adjusted it so that she can use her car to do it. It's nice that there are things between us that haven't faded or been lost.

"I love that you still do that," I tell her as I get in the car.

"What?"

"Flash your lights. You could just call. The way things are now, you could probably honk your horn." And even if anyone was home, they'd probably be too drunk or too preoccupied to notice, I think.

"Huh." She wrinkles her brow. "I've never really thought about it. Habit."

"So why the sudden urge to sneak into the pool?"

"The moon was full, my homework was done, and I missed you."

I crane my neck out the window and look up at the moon, a perfect white disc hanging in the blue-black sky. "Thanks."

"No, no, thank you for coming. So, let's get the history over with and then we'll talk. He's got us doing the Industrial Revolution and the civil rights movement. . . ."

"What?" Mr. Bingler has a habit of jumping around a lot and having us study two completely different periods of history at once. He seems to think he's teaching us these deep, profound lessons about history by doing this. But I usually don't get it. "Why would he put those two together?"

"It's kind of interesting. . . ." Haley talks fast, and by the time we get to the entrance to Olympus Lakes, she's pretty much finished her synopsis. She types a number into the keypad at the security gate and it opens.

Olympus Lakes is a housing development surrounded by man-made lakes on two sides and a golf course on the other two. It was built when I was in fourth grade. In true yuppie fashion, the development has a Greco-Roman theme; most of the homes have columns, and all the streets are named after Greek and Roman gods and goddesses. Navigating through the place is always a treat. "So I turn left on Adonis?" "No, you go past Adonis and Aphrodite to Jupiter, and it's left on Jupiter."

A bunch of new kids moved in and came to our school when it was completed, and my friend Ana, who's on the dance team with me, was one of them. The first time I went over to her house, she took me to the community's clubhouse, which has a huge swimming pool with waterfalls, natural-rock waterslides, three diving boards that are all different heights, and several hot tubs shaded by tropical plants. I was astounded. Back then, everyone else's pools had a deep end, a shallow end, and, if you were lucky, a diving board and/or a hot tub. Haley and I have been sneaking into Olympus Lakes ever since. Now, of course, tons of people have upgraded their pools so that they look like Amazonian lakes, but I still love sneaking in here, although we hardly ever do it anymore.

We skinny-dip because it feels more dangerous, but we only do it when we're sure no one else is around. When I hear about the wild things other girls do, flashing their chests at Mardi Gras, snorting coke at parties, I realize that I am a total dork. But I have to admit, I still feel like a rebel when I skinny-dip in this pool.

Haley and I scale the fence, throw our towels on some plastic lounge chairs, and strip down. We cannonball into the pool, as always, and when we surface, we swim around for a few minutes.

"It's to cold to stay in here long. Let's get in the Jacuzzi," she says, shivering.

"I want to swim a little longer," I tell her.

Haley gets out of the pool and goes to the hot tub, turning on the jets before she gets in. I paddle around the pool a few more times, float on my back for a while, and notice how small my breasts look when I lie on my back. After I am convinced that there is no getting around the fact that they are hopeless, that I will never be featured on a Girls Gone Wild video, I get out of the pool and walk over to the Jacuzzi.

As soon as I sit down, Haley blurts out, "Your brother called me up at two o'clock in the morning last night to ask me to the prom."

"What did you say?"

"I think he was on something."

I wonder if she means that he wasn't just drunk, but high, too. I almost ask, but I worry that Haley won't want to go to the prom with us if she finds out how Allen's been acting lately. "Very funny."

"No, I'm serious."

I avoid looking at her. "He was probably just nervous. What did you say?"

"I told him I'd get back to him. . . . He wasn't just nervous, either." She waits for me to look at her, but I play with the bubbles from the jets instead and pretend that I have no idea what she's getting at.

"So are you going to go with him or what?" I try to seem nonchalant.

"Well, I wanted to ask you what you thought. I mean, I know we'd go with you and Julian, so that would be fun. And I know Al wouldn't pull any Ricky Friedman crap, either. But . . . I don't know. Did you tell him to ask me?" Haley asks.

"He asked you because he wanted to. That's all."

"Okay. Then I'll go with him. But what's the deal with him lately?" Haley moves away from the jet behind her. Her skin gets irritated if she sits in front of it for too long. "We have ceramics together and he hardly ever comes to class. And I swear there was something wrong with him when he called me."

"I think he's been really busy with work, and he coaches Keatie's soccer team with Julian. He was probably just tired."

Haley looks unconvinced.

"Anyway, it's none of our business, right?" I say.

"He's your brother, so it is your business. And I'm your friend, so if your family is having a rough time and you want it to be my business, it can be my business, too. Look, Mia, if you don't want to talk to me about it, that's fine, but if Allen's doing things that could get him, or other people, into serious trouble, someone needs to do something about it."

"You're starting to sound like one of those drug awareness videos they show every year during Red Ribbon Week," I joke. How can I tell her that I can't even deal with my own feelings about my disappearing family and upside-down-inside-out world, much less Allen's?

"I'm sorry," she says, "but I still mean it." She looks at me hard for a moment, to show she really is serious. "Anyway, you and Julian are definitely my business. So what's up with that?"

"I don't know. . . . It seems like things are good." I lean my head back, dip my hair in the water, then wrap it into a knot to keep it out of my face. "Okay so this might be kind of a creepy question, but . . . do you think I have nice boobs?"

"What?" Haley says, her eyes immediately shifting away from me, as if she wants to make sure I know she is not looking at my breasts.

"No, not like that . . . I mean . . . Julian and I kiss. And I like it, don't get me wrong. And we don't necessarily need to do anything else at this point, but isn't he supposed to want to?"

"And you think this has something to do with your boobs?"

"I don't know."

"When you were walking over here from the pool, I thought, 'Mia has great, perky boobs,' in a strictly nonlesbian way, you know."

"Really?"

"Totally. Mine are droopy compared to yours." Haley is beautiful and she has a fantastic body. If I didn't know who her parents were, I'd think she was the love child of a basketball star and a big-breasted supermodel.

"Nah. I was just cold."

We leave when our hands and toes get pruney, and make up questions for Mr. Bingler's homework on the way home. We try to make them sound like textbook questions, but we throw in a few nonsense questions because it's so late and we're sort of out of it.

"How are the effects of the Industrial Revolution apparent in the roots of the civil rights movement?"

"The civil rights movement was not civil, nor did it actually move, but it was right. Discuss."

When Haley drops me off, Allen's car is in the driveway, and the light in his room is off. See, he's fine, in bed by twelve-thirty. When I pass his room on the way to mine, his door is slightly open, but I don't look in.

monopolized

↕

THE CHRISTMAS BEFORE I TURNED NINE, MY GRANDPARENTS, my dad's parents, who've never been great present givers—one year they bought us all new pillows—bought us each a board game. Allen got Monopoly; I got Sorry!; Keatie got Candy Land. I never played mine, but Allen liked his; Keatie was too young to do much more than strew the cards from hers all over the house.

Anyway, that spring we all got the chicken pox. My mom was out of town visiting an old college roommate, and our housekeeper-nanny lady, Prudencia, wouldn't come over because she'd never had chicken pox, so my dad had to stay home from work and take care of us.

It was his idea to play Monopoly.

So we started playing and my dad started talking about

how he hadn't lost a game of Monopoly in twenty-six years or something like that.

"Get ready to lose," Allen told him.

After about three hours of Monopoly I was bored, confused, and almost out of money; Keatie was making towns out of the houses and hotels, pretending to blow them up with the tin top hat game piece that no one had wanted to use; and Dad and Allen were in another galaxy, intent on the game.

I rolled the dice and got an eight, which landed me on a square belonging to Allen that had three houses on it. I counted out almost all my money and gave it to him.

"You got a double," he said. "Two fours, you get to roll again."

"I don't want to," I said. "I'm tired."

"It's the rules." Allen pressed the dice into my hand and closed my fingers around them.

I rolled. Two ones. I moved forward two spaces. Another of Allen's squares; this one had a red plastic hotel on it. I gave Allen the rest of my money.

"That's not enough; you have to mortgage your properties."

"Just take them," I said handing Allen all the cards in my possession.

"All right!"

I began watching TV with Keatie, who'd tired of bombing plastic villages. And then the tide turned.

Smack in the middle of a rerun of *Scooby-Doo* on the Cartoon Network, Allen yelled, "Ye-eah! You are so finished!"

"We'll see," said Dad, with an odd edge to his voice. He counted his money twice. He turned over each of his cards one at a time, adding in his head.

"You don't have enough, Dad," said Allen.

"We'll see," he repeated, writing down numbers on a piece of paper money.

"I beat you. You're done."

Dad calmly picked up the game board and folded it, funneling the pieces on it back into the box. He gathered up his multicolored paper money, put it away, and walked out of the room without saying anything.

Keatie remained entranced by the TV. I watched Allen, mystified. I saw Allen's face crumple as he bowed his head and began putting his money and cards back in the box.

Dad didn't say a direct word to Allen or me for the rest of the day. He still wasn't talking to us when my mom got home from her trip the next day, and by then, Allen wasn't talking, either.

"What's going on here?" said Mom, sensing the tension within minutes of arriving home.

Neither Dad nor Allen spoke.

"Allen beat Dad at Monopoly, and Dad hadn't lost in forty-eight years," I told her. "And now they won't talk."

"What? Don't be ridiculous, Mia." She looked at Dad as if she expected him to debunk my story. He didn't say anything.

"It's true," I insisted.

Her mouth twitched, the way it does when something bothers her but she doesn't want to show it. She looked at the two of them. Allen pursed his lips; Dad looked away.

"Russ, tell me what happened."

Dad shrugged and took Mom's bags down the hall to their room.

"Al, is that true?"

Allen nodded. His face tensed, his eyes got watery, he hung his head.

Mom put her arms around him and said, "It's not that, sweetie. It's not you. It must be something else."

Allen buried his head in her chest and didn't speak.

"He's got a lot on his mind." Mom paused. "I'm glad you beat him," she whispered into his ear.

"Dad's a sore loser, huh, Mom?" I said, wanting to be a part of what was happening between Mom and Allen.

"Shhhhhh," she said to me, her arms around Allen. "Shhhhhh."

A few days passed before Dad and Allen actually talked without Mom around to force them.

happy birthday

"MOM, I WANT DADDY TO COME TO MY BIRTHDAY DINNER." Keatie's announcement surprised us all at dinner on the Thursday before her birthday.

Mom was home, for a change, so we were all at the table at seven o'clock, eating dinner, just like we used to. I was a little annoyed when Keatie brought up Dad; I'd been enjoying the illusion of normalcy.

"Okay, sweetie. It's your birthday. Just call him and tell him when to come." Mom was trying to sound natural and like she didn't really care that Keatie wanted to invite Dad, but I could tell it bugged her.

We have this tradition in my family: on our birthdays, we can have whatever kind of party we want with our friends or whatever—within reason, of course—but on the Sunday before our birthday, we have a party just for the family. Mom makes whatever we want for dinner—once Allen chose octopus just to see if Mom would make it—and Dad makes the cake, or pie, or whichever dessert the birthday child has chosen. This year Keatie was going to have a roller-skating party on the day of her birthday; she'd invited the entire third grade.

"I'm just going to invite Dad, and not Paloma. Dad is part of the family and this is a family party, but Paloma is just a visitor. She can come to my skating party but not the dinner." Keatie paused. "She can't understand most of what we say, and she makes it so Daddy doesn't talk to anyone but her."

"Sounds good," sang Mom through clenched teeth.

Which brings us to tonight, the night of Keatie's birthday dinner. My dad arrives with a German chocolate cake and a new video game for Keatie.

"This cake's from a bakery, Dad. I thought you were going to make one special for me like you always do."

"Sorry, Keat, I didn't have any time. Things are really hectic right now."

"And Allen already has this game, remember? He got it for Christmas. Remember—you tried to tell him it was from Santa," Keatie says. Keatie has known the truth about Santa since she was seven, but my dad is still in denial about Keatie growing up.

Dad gets annoyed. "Well, we'll just have to take it back and exchange it, then."

Dad sits on the couch and talks to Keatie about her skating party while Mom starts setting the table. He's surprised when he finds out that instead of eating in the dining room, we are going to eat at the "homework table" in the family room.

"Keatie wanted to eat in here. She specifically requested that we eat at this table," Mom tells him.

"I don't like the other table," says Keatie. "It's too big. And Mom says Grandpa made this table, so I like it better."

I imagine Dad thinking that without him around, our family traditions and dignity are falling to pieces—a birthday dinner in the family room at the old picnic table Grandpa made? Horror of horrors.

Allen walks in just as Mom and I finish setting the table. Keatie squeals and rushes to him; you'd think they hadn't seen each other in years. Allen hands my mom a carton of ice cream and scoops Keatie up into his arms. "Keater, word up. Are you ready to par-tay?" I notice that he doesn't say anything to Dad.

The dinner is fairly peaceful. Keatie's excited about her skating party; Allen talks about soccer practice and soccer scholarships; Mom and Dad manage to be civil to each other. Everything is fine until Keatie mentions Paloma.

"Is she coming to my party, Daddy? I don't think there's roller-skating in Peru; she'd like it. Chewy says that Toshi, his exchange brother, loves to Rollerblade."

Allen gets angry. "Can we please stop acting like Paloma is some kind of exchange student or tourist or whatever? She's your girlfriend, Dad, and you and Mom are still married, technically. So she's basically your mistress, right?"

Hell breaks loose, right at the dinner table. Mom tries to shush Allen.

Dad starts to yell. "Allen, I've had enough of your lip!"

"And we've had enough of your shit," Allen snaps.

"That's enough, you two," Mom says.

Keatie and I hang our heads and try to keep eating, like nothing is happening. I cut my steak, the same piece, into smaller and smaller pieces.

"I don't have to put up with this," Dad says.

"Oh, but we have to put up with you?" Allen asks.

"No, you don't. I'm leaving."

"Let me help you out, then." Allen gets up from the table, opens the front door, walks over to where Dad is, and pushes him off the bench. I try to make sense of what is happening, but I can't. Things are moving too fast, spinning out of control.

Before anyone can say or do anything, Dad and Allen are on the floor, wrestling. And then Mom is there trying to pull them off each other. Keatie and I sit stunned, frozen at the table.

"It was just one dinner," Mom says to Dad when she's finally separated him and Allen. She brushes the disheveled hair out of her eyes. "Can't we spend one hour as a family without anyone arguing or making a scene? Can't we . . ." Her shoulders begin to shake, and she sinks onto the bench of the homework/picnic/dinner table.

Dad straightens his tie and tucks his shirt in without a word. He ruffles Keatie's hair as he leaves and promises to take her shopping to find a new video game. Allen goes to his room, emerges with his jacket and car keys, and disappears. Keatie wipes the tears from her face and puts her thumb in her mouth while I try to act normal and finish eating; I don't want to leave her, so I wait for Mom to stop crying before I go to my room.

Right there, at that moment, I feel like there are no routines left: no dinner at seven, no *Jeopardy!*, no good-night chats. They've all disappeared. For good, it feels like. I have left the realm of the known and entered uncharted territory. I don't recognize my family anymore.

another step

I PICK UP THE JAR AND MAKE A BIG SHOW OUT OF SHAKING IT and choosing a new slip of paper. *Something nobody knows about you*. Yeah, right. "That one's boring; I'll pick another one." I choose a different piece of paper and read aloud, "*Your favorite thing to do*. Easy. There are two: dance and watch TV."

"So tell me about them."

"I've danced since I was three years old and watched TV since I was born," I begin. "I practice downstairs every day while I watch TV. It's embarrassing, because lots of people think TV is for brain-dead people, but I really like it. Some people say you can't do two things at once, but I'm so used to warming up and stretching that it's easy to do that while I watch. And if I already know a routine, I can practice it while I watch. . . . Sometimes I can change my rhythms to match what's happening on TV. And if there's music playing, I can do my routine along with the music, I just change the way I do the dances, you know? I move more quickly if the music or the scene is fast paced, and I slow myself down and move more balletically if what's happening on TV is slower or sadder or whatever. And for my modern stuff—I choreograph the modern dance for the team. The other girls just want to choreograph these slutty, sexy dances that make them look like strippers-in-training. For the modern stuff, I use a lot of the movements I see on TV. I don't know if you'd recognize them, because they're slightly exaggerated, but when you see how people express emotion through movement on TV, it's easy to translate that into a movement in dance." I take a breath. I've never really tried to explain my dancing to anyone before. Just talking about it, I feel free. Less weighed down. I've never realized before that dancing is safe.

Lisz beams. "I think it's fabulous that you have such a passion and that you've found a way to, um, customize it, to make it your own. Why do you enjoy dance and TV so much?"

"I don't know. I guess I like dance because I've been doing it for so long that it just feels natural, like something I have to do—like eating, or talking. . . . It's an outlet for my energy, I guess. . . . It's like I can express myself in front of people but not have to worry about people thinking I'm crazy or weird. . . . It's like a language all my own that other people can translate and enjoy for themselves, but only I know what it really means to me. I can't really explain it."

"That makes sense to me. I like to paint. I'm not very

good, but I still like to do it. And sometimes other people will see what I paint and really like it, and it feels good, their appreciation of my art. But they still never quite get out of it what I put into it; it's something that I enjoy more than the people who look at my paintings."

"Yeah. It's kinda like that for me with dance."

"What about TV?"

"I don't know. I just think it's interesting to see what's going on in other people's lives and how other people live."

"I'm sure you've heard people say that television is an escape, that it's unrealistic . . . that nobody really lives the lives shown on TV."

"Yeah. I don't know. I've never known anyone from New York City or Beverly Hills. I've never been a doctor in a hospital emergency room. I've never been to Tibet. It seems like I can learn a lot of stuff from TV. About life. And it's better than the boring stuff that goes on in my life." I wonder about what she said about escape. Is it always bad to escape? Do we always have to just hang around staring our problems in the face?

"You think your life is boring?"

"Not always. But it's just really interesting to me to see how other people live, how they feel, how they react to things. I like it. Maybe it is an escape, but it's pretty tough to escape what is real in my own life and what isn't." It's pretty tough to ignore the fact that your brother, who may have been drunk, tried to beat up your dad, who is apparently no more mature than a seventeen-year-old.

play ball

Among the three of them, Keatie, Allen, and Julian have asked 98 percent of the free world to attend Yorba United's first soccer game. Still, Mom and I are surprised when Dad and Paloma show up and plant their lawn chairs a few feet from ours on the grass. Paloma spots me and says hello.

"Ay, Mia, how you are?"

"*Muy bien, gracias*. How are you?"

"Very good. I love to watch the, eeehhhh, soccer. I am happy to see Keatie play."

Dad, ever oblivious, doesn't realize what he's done, the uncomfortable position he's put everyone in, until he sees Mom.

"Well, uh, Maggie. Hello."

She stands up and walks over. "How are you, Russ?"

"Doing well. . . . Do you, uh, have you, uh, made the acquaintance of my, uh, Paloma?"

"No, I haven't." Mom seems to be enjoying Dad's discomfort.

"Well, uh, Paloma, this is, uh, Maggie, *mi esposa. Bueno, mi* ex-*esposa.*"

"Oh, yes. Maggie. Is good to meet you. I am Paloma."

"It's nice to meet you, too. Thank you for coming to Keatie's game."

"Oh, yes. I love the game," Paloma says, smiling.

They all stand there, grimacing awkwardly. I decide to rescue them.

"Mom, can I get the blanket out of the car? It's a little bit chilly."

"Of course. The keys are in my purse." She returns to our chairs and begins digging through her purse.

"Dad, you should probably sit on the other side of the field next time. Especially if you're going to bring Paloma. Just so things aren't so creepy," I tell him.

"Oh . . . right." He looks more annoyed than embarrassed.

The game is eventful. Keatie scores a goal. So does her friend Chewy. Paloma really seems to enjoy herself. She yells out what I assume is encouragement in Spanish to Keatie until halftime, when Keatie asks Dad to tell her to stop. Dad reads a book for most of the game, calling out, "Nice work, Keatie!" or "Way to play!" whenever Paloma nudges him.

The team is up by one goal until the last ten minutes of the game, during which the other team scores twice. At this point, Keatie kicks Mason, her teammate, for not blocking one of the goals. Because of this she gets a red card, a penalty for unsportsmanlike behavior, which means she can't play for the rest of the game. This causes Allen to go crazy.

"He's on her team," Allen yells at the ref. "We're okay with kicking on this team. We let 'em kick each other. You can't red-card her for kicking someone on her own team."

That, of course, upsets Mason's father, who gets up in Allen's face for not protecting his kid.

"Your kid can't play. He sucks. What do you want me to do about that? We're here to win games," Allen yells at him. Which begins a brief yelling match, which ends with Allen's being escorted off the field, which causes several concerned parents to approach Julian after the game and ask if Allen's temper is always an issue.

When Mom brings out a big cooler of orange slices and juice boxes and hands them out to Keatie's teammates, Keatie tries to convince Mom that Mason should not be allowed to have his, but Mom gives him his drink and orange slices anyway. Once snacks have been distributed, Mom takes Allen aside and gives him a lecture. "I honestly don't know what has gotten into you," she says. "Sweetie, what is your problem?"

Allen shrugs, mumbles something.

I wait and watch, hoping my mom will figure it out. I want her to see through him and just know, the way she always seemed to know what was wrong when I was little. I at least want her to show that she knows how to ask real questions and get real answers. But she doesn't. Not this time.

"You need to get this under control, Allen." She ruffles his hair and smiles. Then her cell phone rings. She looks at it and says, "I need to take this call. But this conversation is not over." She's wrong; it is. She flips open the phone and walks away. When she does, I catch a glimpse of Allen's face. He looks like a little boy; he looks hurt and scared.

Somewhere in the middle of the chaos, Dad and Paloma left. They didn't say goodbye or good game, they just left. "Typical," my mom says when I point this out to her.

penciled in

MY MOM CALLS ME TO SCHEDULE A TIME TO GO SHOPPING FOR a prom dress.

"How about Friday after school? From two-thirty to five-thirty?" she asks.

"Okay. I guess that's fine. Can Haley come, too?"

"Well, I wanted to see you and have it be just the two of us . . ." She pauses, waiting for me to say something.

I want Haley to come, but I don't want to hurt Mom's feelings. I wait.

"But Haley's practically family, so I guess that's fine."

"Okay, I'll ask her. . . . She might not even be able to come."

"I'm going to have Suzanne schedule this, though, so even

if Haley can't come, are we still on?" Suzanne is her new assistant.

The day Mom told us about Suzanne, she was so excited. "Now I'll be able to be at home more again," she told us. But every parent I know who has an assistant is never home. And it's usually their assistants who call to tell the kids not to wait up.

But back to the issue at hand. Shopping. Mom is waiting for an answer. "Yeah, sure," I say.

I have an appointment to go shopping with my mother. I wonder if I should start scheduling more time with her—maybe that's how I'm supposed to do things now. Maybe I just missed the memo.

lives in jeopardy

I AM ON THE PHONE IN MY BEDROOM TALKING TO HALEY, AND I hear noise coming from down the hall. Keatie and Allen are arguing, which almost never happens.

"I'll call you back in a minute, Haley."

I walk out to the living room and find Keatie standing in front of the TV, blocking Allen's view of it, crying.

"What's going on?" I ask.

"I'm trying to watch TV and Keater's freaking out," Allen tells me.

"He's trying to watch *Seinfeld*," Keatie sobs.

"What's wrong with that?" I ask her.

"It's not *Jeopardy!*" she says. "In this family we watch *Jeopardy!* at seven-thirty."

"I don't feel like watching freaking *Jeopardy!*" Allen says.

"Mia, tell him," Keatie begs.

I can see what's going on. Things I am afraid to see are laid out in front of me in Keatie's scared, sad face. If we don't watch *Jeopardy!*, she thinks, that's it. Everything is gone. Keatie finally sees what's happened, and she's trying to hold on to what she knows, what's left of certainty, and for her, it's *Jeopardy!*

"Allen, please, just watch *Jeopardy!* It's what we've always done. She just wants things to be normal, you know. For her, *Jeopardy!* makes things normal."

"I am *not* watching *Jeopardy!*" he says. After a brief pause, he adds, "There is no more normal here."

When Keatie hears this, she sinks to the floor. The energy drains from her body. When she looks up at me, her face is blank.

dressing-room drama

ON FRIDAY, MOM PICKS ME AND HALEY UP AFTER SCHOOL right on schedule. She kisses us both on the cheek as we get into the car.

"Where do you want to go?" she asks.

"Fashion Island," I tell her. "It's got the best stores."

"Fashion Island it is, then," she says.

I turn on the radio, looking for a good station. Mom gets a call on her cell phone and turns the music off. I try to talk to Haley about the state tennis tournament (she's ranked third in the entire state this year), but my mom shushes me, so we sit and listen to her talk about the Ravenberger account, whatever that is, for the twenty-seven minutes it takes us to get to the mall. When we pull into the parking lot, Mom asks if she can call the person back "in five."

Mom talks on the phone from store to store to store, nodding at the dresses she likes, making faces at the ones she doesn't.

"Who's the obnoxious lady on the phone and what has she done with your mother?" Haley whispers as we examine the fabric of a red lace dress.

"I have no idea, but I'm so glad to be getting some quality mother-daughter-Ravenberger bonding time in. I was feeling so deprived. I'd almost forgotten how much the Ravenbergers mean to me." I am wondering the same thing as Haley, though: Who is this woman? And, more importantly, why did she make such a big deal about this whole dress-buying thing if she was just going to talk to someone else the entire time?

We put three dresses on hold at three different stores. Mom finally gets off the phone while we are at Nordstrom.

Because Mom's been on the phone, Haley and I have set up a routine of trying on all the dresses we pick and only showing her the ones we like so we don't have to interrupt her as much. So when we find the perfect dress—a black backless spaghetti-strapped one that barely zips up but looks damn good on—we have agreed that it is *the Dress* before Mom has even seen it. Haley goes out to the racks to find my mother, who has taken it upon herself to pick out some dresses for me, too.

"Maggie, we've found it," I hear Haley saying as she leads Mom back to the dressing room. "It's *the Dress*."

When Mom enters the dressing room and sees me in the

Dress, she drops her pile of pink, lilac, and baby blue gowns on the floor, sinks onto the dressing room bench, and closes her eyes.

Haley looks at me, confused. I look at her and shrug. We both watch Mom, waiting for some kind of clue as to what is going on. She opens her eyes; they are red and teary.

"Do you like it?" I ask.

Mom looks at me, at the Dress. "That's the dress you want to wear?" she asks, her voice tight.

"I think so," I say.

"It's the best one she's tried on," says Haley.

Mom doesn't say anything for a while.

"You look like a slut," she finally says.

"What?" My mother has never called me a slut before. She's never really made any comments about my clothes, except to tell me I look nice or to let me know when I've left a tag on or something. She's never seemed to care what I wear. I mean, I don't usually wear halter tops and miniskirts or anything like that to school, but I don't wear baggy sweatsuits, either. Sometimes I wear sexy-ish clothes, sometimes I don't.

"You're fifteen years old," she says.

"Almost sixteen," I remind her.

"You are fifteen years old," she repeats. "You're just a little girl and you want to wear that? You want to go out in public like that? When did this happen?"

Haley looks scared. I am scared. I have no idea what is going on. And why is she calling me a little girl?

"What's wrong with the dress? It's long. It's not even strapless. It's not like my boobs are falling out of it. Mom, you're acting crazy."

She stands up. "I will not buy you a dress like that, Mia. You are not an adult, you are not a prostitute, and you aren't going to dress like one. Find something else." She hands me the pile of pastel gowns she dropped on the floor and leaves the dressing room.

"What just happened?" whispers Haley.

"I have no idea."

We leave the mall twenty minutes later carrying a pale pink dress with cap sleeves and a long, straight skirt, the dress Mom liked best, which, compared with the black dress, strongly resembles a pink Hefty bag.

I suspect that some strange alien workaholic nun has possessed my mother's body. Because she is not in her right mind, I can't be expected to do what she wants me to, right? Desperate times call for desperate measures, so I resort to emergency tactics, more specifically the old ask-the-parent-who-is-more-likely-to-give-you-what-you-want-and-leave-the-other-one-out-of-it maneuver.

I call Dad after Mom drops us off; she has to go back to work to handle some kind of crisis. "I was wondering if you could take me shopping for a prom dress. Mom doesn't have enough time to go with me."

On Saturday my dad picks me up thirty minutes later than the time we agreed on, and Paloma is in the car with him. I sit in the backseat while Dad and Paloma chat in Spanish. From what I understand, and from the frequent mention of the word *prom*, I gather that he is telling her how prom works. When we get to the mall, I lead them straight to the black dress. I try it on, just to make it seem like I am really shopping.

"¡*Ay!* Sexy!" Paloma says.

"Pretty, uh, grown-up, Mia," Dad says. "What would your mother say?"

"I think she'd like it, actually."

He looks doubtful.

"Okay, so when she sees it, she'll probably get all emotional about how I'm growing up. You know how she is. . . . But I'm sure she'll be fine with it." I realize I am overexplaining, which Allen has taught me is the number one giveaway when you're telling a lie.

"Well . . . Are you sure you don't want to try anything else on?"

"No. I like this one. And I know you probably have lots to do, right? And we don't want Paloma to get bored." I feel a teensy bit guilty about all this, and I just want to get the dress and get out of here. When I was younger, my mom could always tell I was lying just by looking at my face; I always thought she had some kind of psychic superpower. I don't think my dad has the same ability, but I avoid looking him in the eye, just in case.

"We're in no rush, Mia. Paloma enjoys shopping, and we've got plenty of time. I think this is the first time we've spent any time together since your mom and I . . ." He trails off, uncomfortable.

"Yeah. But, really, this dress is great. I want to get it. And I haven't finished my chores yet, so . . ."

"Okay, well, then let's get it."

We're in and out of the mall in half an hour, no tears.

I don't know how I'll be able to wear the Dress without Mom's knowing, or how I'll convince Mom to let me wear it, but I do know that I will not be wearing a pink Hefty bag to my prom.

islands

↕

I AM SITTING IN MY ROOM ALONE, NOT DOING ANYTHING, JUST lying on my bed and thinking. I hear music coming from Keatie's room; she is playing her violin. I didn't even know she was home. I want to let her know that I am home, that I can hear her, but I don't want to interrupt her practice. She plays everything slow. Like a funeral march. I barely recognize "Turkey in the Straw."

overheard

My cell phone goes dead while I'm talking to Ana about the costumes for our new competition piece. I pick up the landline phone in my room to call her back and I hear Mom's voice.

"... going through a negative phase right now, though."

"I did the same thing when I was that age," replies a familiar voice.

"I've been so worried about Allen that I haven't really thought about her until we went shopping for her prom dress. You should've seen the stuff she was trying on; it looked like lingerie. I would've put a stop to her prom date right then and there if it weren't for the fact that she's going with Julian."

"He's a good kid, but there's no telling when his father's

genes will manifest themselves." The voice belongs to Julian's mom.

"Oh, please, he's an angel. Mia, though, she's all over the place. Sweet one minute, not talking the next. I have a hard time knowing what she thinks. She never talks about the divorce, hasn't asked me about it. . . . She acts like nothing has happened half the time."

"She seems fine when she's over here. She's so cute with Julian; she'll sit for hours just watching him play video games."

"I hope she doesn't smother the poor kid."

I can't believe what I'm hearing. My mother thinks I am some sort of pathetic smotherer. Does Julian think so, too? Does everyone?

"Oh, Julian eats it up."

"What about you? How are things going with Rick?"

"You won't believe this. He's been talking about getting married. Can you believe it?"

"*Hope!* That's wonderful. How do you feel about that?"

I press the On/Off button on the phone.

breakfast + lunch = brunch

DAD INVITES US FOR SUNDAY BRUNCH AT HIS HOUSE.

Mom says we have to go. "He's your father and you need to have a relationship with him. If you have issues with him, you need to discuss them. You can't just act like he doesn't exist."

I love it when my mom gives advice that seems completely contradictory to the way she actually behaves and the way she raised us. She's always told us not to waste our time on things we don't enjoy or find rewarding just for the sake of appearance or because of some ridiculous societal expectation or tradition, and now she seems to be telling us to do just that.

Technically, we're supposed to be with Dad every Tuesday night and every other weekend, but nobody has really tried to enforce this. Allen hasn't spoken to Dad since the birthday brawl. I haven't been avoiding Dad—not on purpose, at least—but it's harder to find a time or a reason to talk to him now that he lives in another house. Keatie calls him all the time; I think she kind of enjoys the novelty of having a parent who has been relieved of disciplinary duties, who lives somewhere else, and who takes her out to eat a lot.

On Sunday, Allen drives.

Dad and Paloma make eggs Benedict.

Keatie asks if she can get a dog and keep it at Dad's condo.

I feel like I'm not even there, like I'm having one of those dreams where you're watching things happen but you aren't a part of them, and you're there, but no one can see you or hear you—maybe you're invisible, maybe everyone else is just too busy to see you. I watch and wonder. In my head I ask brave questions: Since when is this my family? Since when does my dad cook meals? Sure, he's great with baked goods, but real food? And since when is he a brunch eater? Since when does he stand so close to a woman who isn't my mother? Since when does Keatie want a dog? Since when does Allen just sit and watch TV?

I notice my dad's old viola case leaning against his new, perfect-for-a-single-guy's-condo couch; I wonder if he's started playing again. The last time I saw the viola was when he tried to convince me to take it up and play in the junior high school orchestra; he got it out and showed me how to play a G.

"See, Mia, that wasn't hard. You can play already."

I tried out for cheerleading instead.

"Eees rrready," Paloma says as she enters the room carrying a pitcher of juice.

"Everybody have a seat," Dad yells from the kitchen.

Keatie and I sit down at the table obediently. Allen ignores Dad and continues to watch TV until Dad comes in and turns it off.

"We're ready to eat now, son."

Son? Since when does Dad call Allen *son*?

I'm not the only one who notices this.

"Okay, *Father*," Allen says, his voice tight, taking his time getting up and sauntering over to the table before he finally sits down.

Paloma beams as if she has just put the last piece of a jigsaw puzzle in place and can finally see the whole, perfect picture.

"Shall we bless the meal?" Dad asks. We say grace before meals on rare occasions in our home: when my grandparents are there, and on holidays.

Allen smirks and opens his mouth to say something, but Keatie cuts him off.

"Can I say grace?" she pleads.

Like anyone else is going to volunteer.

I don't shut my eyes while she prays about dogs, families, soccer, and eggs. Instead, I survey the scene. Even though it's a different table, everyone sits in the same places they did at our house, only Paloma sits where Mom usually does. Allen doesn't close his eyes, either; he keeps them fixed on Keatie through the entire prayer.

While we are eating, quietly and awkwardly, Dad pipes up, "Well, Mia, Paloma was so intrigued by my explanation of your prom while we were shopping the other day that I decided she should see one herself. And your school actually sent out a request for chaperones on the parent e-mail list. So we've volunteered. Paloma and I are going to help chaperone the dance."

My jaw drops; I am speechless. My dad is coming to my prom? My *dad* is coming to my prom? I feel like the kid in that story, the one who put his finger in the dam to keep it from breaking and flooding his town, only it feels like my finger has gotten stuck in the dam, which has burst anyway, and I am drowning.

"I like very much to dance," says Paloma, excited to join the conversation. "In Peru I am a dancer in the Ballet Nacional."

Paloma is a dancer? Like me? Perfect. I picture myself wearing a tutu and floating facedown in a flooded village while my dad and Paloma drift by in a lifeboat.

"There is no way you are going to chaperone my prom with your girlfriend," Allen tells Dad, looking at me as if this is all my fault.

"Can I come, too?" Keatie begs.

"I've made a commitment to your school, Allen. And I think that it would be good for me to be more participative when it comes to the lives of my children."

"It's a little late for that, Dad," Allen retorts.

Paloma looks disappointed, embarrassed. She hangs her

head. She dances, like me. Maybe she feels lost in this family, like me, like all of us.

On one of the first days of ninth grade, all the freshmen had to attend an assembly that was supposed to teach us tactics for surviving in high school. One of the things Ms. Hooten, the vice principal, told us to do was to make lists to stay organized and keep from falling behind in homework or missing important extracurricular events. Sometimes I make lists to remember what I'm supposed to do on a given day or to make sure I have everything in my backpack before I leave for school.

When I get home, I make a list to make sense of my father and his brunch, to organize everything that seems strange about them in my mind.

(1) lives in a one-bedroom condo with a Peruvian woman he has known for a month—even though he is still married to my mother.

(2) says prayers before he eats—even though he used to grumble when my mother asked him to bless the food or say grace before meals.

(3) plays the viola.

(4) wants to go to my prom.

But some things are too complicated to put on a list, and some I can't put into words at all.

I'M SUPPOSED TO HAVE AT LEAST A VERSION OF NEXT YEAR'S modern dance competition piece ready by May 15, so that when we audition new girls for the dance team we know whether they can handle it. The thing is, every time I try to work through it, I get distracted.

I am a minute thirty into the routine when I notice my fingernails. They're dirty. How do nails get dirty if you bathe regularly and you aren't a mechanic or a construction worker? So I have to stop dancing and do my nails, because now that I know they're dirty I can't think of anything else.

my dream prom

MY RADIO ALARM GOES OFF AND I WAKE TO A DJ DOING AN Arnold Schwarzenegger impression and discussing something political. It's hard to take the government seriously when the Terminator runs your state. I hit the snooze button.

In the silence, a piece of the dream I was having floats into my head. I was at the prom wearing my mother's wedding dress and my dad was my date; Paloma was there with Julian, wearing my prom dress. Everyone at the dance was wounded, blood soaking their tuxedo shirts and formal dresses. They were all missing pieces of their body. Julian only had one leg, Paloma had a huge hole in her chest, Dad was missing an arm. Half of Kiki Nordgren's face was gone. I was whole, though. I try to remember why. And then it comes back. I wasn't whole. I was missing my entire body. I was a ghost.

The dream disturbs me. Thinking about it, I realize that I would rather have a gaping bloody wound than be nothing at all.

Later on, I remember something else: I wasn't just a ghost, I was carrying their missing pieces. Maybe I was the one who had taken them.

spilling my guts

↕

Two days before the prom I am in Lisz's office for my weekly appointment. I can't stop thinking about my dream. I feel like a ghost again, only now I feel as if I'm drowning, too.

"Can I ask you a question?" I say, pushing the question jar to the side.

"Sure," Lisz says.

"Do you think I'm a future serial killer, or a suicide case, or something?"

"Mia, you can't be serious."

"I am, though."

"No. I absolutely do not."

"Oh." I feel relieved, like I've come up for air.

"Can I ask you a question?" Lisz asks.

"Depends on the question," I tell her.

"Why would you think you might be a serial killer?"

"Well, I had this dream. . . ." I start to tell her. I hesitate, wondering what I should leave out. I realize that I am too tired to leave things out and try to remember them all. So I tell her everything. I tell her about my dream. I tell her about finding Allen hungover. I tell her about Julian and my boobs.

And she listens.

"So?" I say when I am finished. "What do you think?"

"I think you have a lot of weight on your shoulders. Too much. And I think you put some of it there when you don't need to, and I think some other people put it there when they shouldn't."

"So what should I do?" I ask. I mean, I finally told the truth, so she got what she wanted. Now she can do her magic or whatever. Now she can give me her answers.

"That's what we're finally going to be able to figure out," she tells me.

"That's it?"

"For now, that's it. You've got a beginning." She acts like I've just been crowned Miss America.

"That's it? A beginning?"

"I think it's what we've been waiting for," she says.

I decide to believe her. For now. I'll give Lisz maybe a chapter a week—not the whole story, but some if it—and I'll see if it works.

baby day

THE MORNING AFTER KEATIE WAS BORN I WORE A T-SHIRT TO school that had the words BIG SISTER on it in big pink letters. I felt like having someone in the family who was younger than me made me a more important part of my family. I finally had someone to take care of, just like everyone else.

"My mom had our baby," I announced to my class at school. "Yesterday."

My teacher, Ms. Plummer, asked me to wait until announcements to tell the class my "exciting news."

When it was time, Ms. Plummer asked me to come to the front of the class to tell about the baby.

"She has brown hair and she weighs nine pounds and one ounce. And she is going to live at our house." Ms. Plummer wrote the information on the board.

"What is your sister's name?" she asked.

"We don't have one yet. We thought she was a boy. Then when she came out, the doctor saw that she didn't have a—"

"I see. Well, when you know her name, be sure to let us know. For now we'll just call her Baby." Ms. Plummer wrote *Baby Day* on the board above the words *brown hair* and *9 lbs. 1 oz.*

Mom was so used to having just Allen and me that once, after Keatie was born, she almost forgot about her and left her at home. She got into the car, made sure Allen and I were buckled up, and almost left; luckily, she noticed Keatie's empty car seat when she looked in the rearview mirror while she was backing out. Another reason I need to be better about using my mirrors when I drive, I suppose. If I don't get into the habit, my future children's lives could be at stake.

For a while after that, I worried that my mom would forget me, too. But I got over it when I talked to Allen about it.

"Duh, Mia," he said. "We're the ones she remembered."

Thinking about that now, though, thinking about Keatie stuck in front of the music academy and Allen left alone on the sidelines after that disastrous soccer game, I wonder if she has, in some ways, forgotten us.

prom day

I WAKE UP AT ELEVEN AND THERE ARE ALREADY THREE MESsages on my phone.

Mom: "Mia, it's me. I had to go into work early this morning, but I wanted to call and find out what time you'd be leaving so I can be there when you and Allen go. And let me know if you need any help getting ready or if you need me to bring anything home. I forgot pantyhose on the night of my prom. Back then, everyone still wore them, so it was a big deal. Call me when you get this, honey."

Julian: "Today's the day. I have a few questions for you, so call me."

Haley: "Mia, your brother just called and told me that he isn't going to the prom. Please tell me this is some kind of joke."

get the message

↕

I WALK DOWN THE HALL TO ALLEN'S ROOM. HE ISN'T THERE. I call his cell phone; he doesn't pick up. I leave a message; it takes significant effort for me to restrain myself from screaming into the phone. "Al, it's me. Haley thinks you aren't taking her to the prom anymore. You can't just back out of a prom date the day of the prom. If you need money or something, ask Mom or Dad. And please call me back. And you *are* taking Haley. Where are you, anyway?"

I call Mom. I get her voice mail.

"Hi, this is Maggie Preston. . . ."

Since when does she go by her maiden name? She's not even divorced yet.

"I can't take your call right now, but if you'll leave your name and phone number, I'll get back to you as soon as I can.

If your call is urgent, press zero and you'll be forwarded to my assistant." Instead of a beep, there's an odd medley of ringing bells.

"Mom, it's me. I'm getting ready at Haley's. We'll take pictures, okay? Have you seen Allen? I can't find him, and I need to talk to him about tonight. Bye."

I call Julian. "Allen's gone. And he told Haley he isn't going to prom."

"Yeah, I know."

"You do?"

"He was over here last night and he got pretty crazy."

"What do you mean?"

"I don't know. I'm not getting into this. You should just talk to Al yourself."

What? Since when was Julian so . . . diplomatic?

"Oh. Right. What was I thinking, asking you? I mean, *we* aren't friends or anything. We just hang out once in a while and make out sometimes. Why would I ever presume to ask you about my brother?"

"Are you kidding? C'mon, Meems. Any time I say anything about Allen's problems, you make some excuse or say that I must be wrong."

"I don't know what you're talking about."

"Okay. I must've misinterpreted things. I'm really tired. Can I call you later?"

"Sure. Whatever. I've got a million things to do, too."

"All right, then I'll talk to you later. Bye."

"See ya."

I call Haley.

"Thank goodness it's you!" she exclaims when she answers the phone. "What is going on? Please tell me that I am still going to the prom."

"I'm working on that."

"What is it, Mia? Has he been drinking? Is it something else?"

"I don't know. I have no idea what the deal is. He freaked out when my dad told us he was going to chaperone the dance, but I didn't think he would—"

"Have you talked to your mom about what he's been doing?"

"Are you kidding? What am I supposed to say? Look, it'll work out. I know he's not really going to skip the prom; he wouldn't do that to you. I'm going to come over in an hour to get ready. It's going to be fine."

"You always think everything is going to be fine. Sometimes it isn't."

"Well, this time it is."

"I hope so. I'll see you in an hour."

I HEAR THE MOVIE PLAYING BEFORE I SEE IT.

"Another round please, bartender." Allen's slurred voice floats from the TV.

Keatie is at it again, watching home movies.

This one is of all of us cleaning up after a New Year's Eve party my parents threw a few years ago. Allen has picked up some empty champagne bottles, one in each hand, and is pretending to be drunk. He staggers around the room.

"Whoa, this room is really spinning," he says, pretending to take another drink from the bottle as he stumbles around the room. "Guess I don't have my sea legs yet."

I grab the remote from Keatie and turn off the TV.

"Hey," she says. "I was watching that."

"Would you stop watching those stupid movies?" I shout. "What's wrong with you?" I throw the remote on the couch and stomp back to my room.

dress rehearsal

THE GUYS ARE SUPPOSED TO PICK US UP IN TWO HOURS, AND I am beginning to panic. Not that it's ever taken me that long to get ready for anything in my entire life. Haley and I are wearing bathrobes; we've just finished painting our toenails.

"Haley, do you have time to do that thing with my hair where you make those spiral curls . . . you know, like what's-her-name from that movie?"

"I thought you were wearing it straight."

"Well, now I wonder if curly hair would be sexier."

"Meems, my hair is still wet. Do you realize this?"

"Yeah, but . . ."

"But what?" She begins to dry her hair with a towel. "You know, you've been acting like this whole night is about you, Mia. This is my prom, too. Did you bother to come with me to pick out my dress? No, you didn't. I had to take a cold shower because you were in there forever and *you* used all the hot water. I agree to go to the prom with your brother, and now he may not even show up. And all you can think about is your hair. I'm supposed to be your best friend, Mia, and you're treating me like I'm your maid."

I haven't seen Haley this upset since the time her mom made her start eating red meat again because she was iron deficient. I feel like a total jerk.

"Haley . . . I'm so sorry. I didn't realize . . ."

"You don't realize a lot of things. At least, you act like you don't. And I'm not just talking about the way you've been acting like you're the star of prom. I'm talking about your family crap, too." She rubs the towel against her head so vigorously that it looks like she's trying to start a fire.

"Look, I'm sorry about the prom stuff. I've been a total brat, you're right. Let's just drop it and start over. . . . I'll do my own hair. And you should be careful with that towel, you're not going to have any hair left when you finish." I give Haley the most apologetic look I can muster.

"You're damned right, you'll do your own hair." She puts down the towel, goes to the bathroom across the hall from her room, gets out a hair dryer, turns it on, and shuts the door.

I decide to leave her alone for a while.

I call Julian to ask him if he's heard from Allen.

"We're picking up your flowers right now. Al's a little, uh, funny, but everything's going to work out."

Allen gets on the phone. "Tell Haley that I am going to

show her the time of her life," he says, slurring his words.

I can hear Julian struggling to take the phone back.

"We'll be there at six-thirty or so."

"Okay. . . . Are you sure everything's all right?"

"No. But we'll be there at six-thirty. See you then."

I remember what Lisz told me during our appointment this week.

"Ignoring a problem will never make it go away, Mia. Sooner or later things come to a head. Sooner or later you have to deal with them."

Things can come to a head tomorrow. "Tonight I am a princess," I repeat to myself over and over again, until I realize it sounds crazy.

When Haley comes out of the bathroom, she seems relaxed.

I decide not to mention the explosion.

She sits down in front of her mirror and starts to do her makeup. I decide to do my hair myself, but after seven minutes of struggling with the curling iron, I'm ready to give up.

"Okay, princess," Haley says (she couldn't have heard that, could she?), "let's do your hair like what's-her-name's."

"Thank you."

Haley does my hair; I help her with her makeup; things seem normal again.

At six-twenty we put our dresses on and Haley's mom takes pictures of us; I almost call my mom to tell her to come and see us and take pictures, too, but then I remember about the dress. Haley's mom tells me I look beautiful, but it's not the same.

elvis has left the building

SIX-FIFTY-TWO P.M. ALLEN AND JULIAN ARRIVE TO PICK UP Haley and me. Allen is wearing a powder blue tuxedo.

"I tried to talk him out of it," Julian tells us.

"This is a rock star suit," Allen says, "and Haley is my supermodel date."

Haley's mom gives us a confused look. We both shrug.

"I promise to take excellent care of your daughter. And I will tell you right now that I do not plan on trying to seduce her," Allen tells her.

"Well . . . thank you . . ." She looks worried.

"He's just kidding, Mom," Haley tells her.

Her mom snaps some pictures and tells us three times before we leave to have fun and be careful.

boogie nights

We eat dinner at a fancy French restaurant. Al orders escargots and makes us all try one. They're actually pretty good, a little garlicky, though. He tries to order a bottle of wine, too. But the waiter doesn't go for it.

"Maybe in a few years," he tells Allen.

Haley keeps looking at me funny throughout dinner. I check to make sure my boobs aren't falling out of my dress or anything. I give her "What?" looks, but I can't figure out what she's trying to say.

We get lost on the way to the dance because it's being held at a reception center nobody's ever been to before. We arrive just after the king and queen have been crowned. Kiki Nordgren rushes by us in tears, so I assume she didn't win.

"Hey, Kik," Al yells after her, "I voted for you," at which she sobs loudly.

"So *intense*," Al says to no one in particular.

I am a princess, I think. I'm going to have a perfect prom.

"Mia, bathroom," Haley orders.

"We're going to go freshen up before pictures," I tell Julian.

We follow a stream of guyless girls to the restroom.

In the bathroom, Haley grabs my shoulders; her hands are ice cold. "Mia, your brother is drunk. If he gets caught at the prom drunk, he could get kicked out of school."

"He can't be drunk; the waiter wouldn't bring us any wine, remember?"

"Hello. Earth to Mia. He was drunk by the time he got to my house. And I have a feeling he's been drinking all night. He went to the bathroom three times during dinner. I think he has a flask or some minibottles with him."

I remember the canteen I found. "Well, what am I supposed to do?" I ask her. This is not happening. I do not have to deal with this. This is my prom. It's going to be perfect. My drunk brother is going to behave himself and everything is going to work out.

"I don't know. Your dad and the Slut are chaperoning, right?"

"Actually, she might not be a total slut—she liked my dress, which is more than I can say for my mom. . . ."

"Stay with me, here. Now isn't the ideal time to reevaluate your opinion of your dad's girlfriend. We need to find your dad and ask him to take Allen home."

"Allen will not go anywhere with my dad. And my dad would completely flip out if he found out about Al."

"Then we need to take him home."

"If we take him home, we'll miss the whole dance. Let's go back out there, see how he's doing, and ask him what he wants to do."

"All right. But we really have to come up with a plan. You can't just take off with Julian and leave me with your drunk brother."

"I promise we'll make a plan."

When we get back to the dance, Al and Julian are in line for pictures. The second we join them, Haley nudges me.

I blurt out, "Al, listen . . . Haley thinks you're drunk."

Haley's jaw drops.

"And I do, too," I add.

"Allen! Mia!" My dad's voice booms.

We turn and see my dad and Paloma making their way toward us, waving their arms wildly.

"Shit," Allen says.

"We've been looking all over for you," Dad tells us.

"We haven't been looking anywhere for you," Al tells him.

Please, not here. Not now. I am a princess.

"Mia, Haley, you look beautiful," Dad tells us, without acknowledging Allen's comment.

"Thanks," we chorus.

I look at Paloma so I can return the compliment, and I notice her dress. She is wearing my dress, just like in my dream.

Well, not my dress exactly, but a red version of my dress. I stare. She has great boobs.

"Actually, Dad, I was just kidding when I said we weren't looking for you," Allen says. "We just didn't expect you to show up on time. Like usual."

Dad looks hard at Allen, his face shocked, angry. "Have you been drinking?"

"Since I was born."

"Allen, have you been drinking alcohol tonight?" Dad demands.

"You're up," the photographer calls to us.

"Showtime," Allen says, herding us over to the photo corner.

"This discussion is not over," Dad calls after us.

The photographer poses the four of us, counts to three, snaps a picture, and moves Allen and Haley off to the side so that he can take a picture of just Julian and me. He tells Julian to pick me up, like he's carrying me over the threshold or something. Julian pretends that I am too heavy to lift, and the photographer snaps the picture as he is pretending to grimace in pain while he lifts me off the ground.

"Next couple." The photographer motions to Allen and Haley.

"Wait," I plead. "Can't we take another picture? He was joking around and making a weird face."

"Sorry," says the photographer, "better luck next time. Next, please."

Allen drags Haley over and picks her up, like Julian did for our picture. "We're ready," he tells the photographer.

Haley looks completely uncomfortable.

"Whoops, that was the end of the roll," the photographer tells them. "You'll have to wait a minute while I reload the camera."

Allen staggers a bit.

"Al, put me down until he's ready, okay?" Haley begs.

"No, I've got you," he tells her. He looks a little pale.

"All right, all set," says the photographer. "One . . . two . . . three."

As he snaps the photo, Allen falls to his knees and vomits all over Haley.

Dad has been watching the whole scene from across the room. When Allen pukes, Dad grabs Paloma's arm and heads for the door.

"Well, so much for being an involved parent," I say to no one in particular. "When the going gets tough, I guess my dad gets going. Great."

Instead of consulting Allen about a plan, we decide to take matters into our own hands. Julian helps Allen out to the car while Haley and I head back to the bathroom to clean the puke off her dress.

"I'm so sorry," I tell her over and over again.

"Mia, just shut up," she says.

My cell phone rings. It's Dad.

"Where are you? Paloma and I went to get the car, to get Al

out of there, and when I came back in, you were already gone."

"Al's waiting in our car with Julian, and Haley and I are cleaning up."

"I think it's best if I discuss this with your brother and take him home."

"Dad, we've got it," I say, and hang up. I turn off my phone; I refuse to be Dad and Allen's relationship counselor.

When Haley and I get to the car, we find Kiki talking to Allen and Julian.

"He needs to eat something and stay awake," she says.

"If he eats anything, he'll just puke," I tell her.

"If he eats, the food will help absorb the alcohol in his stomach," she says.

"How do you know?"

"It's what I do for my mom," she says quietly. "Believe me, I know."

"Oh."

"Just keep him awake, okay?" Kiki asks if she can come with us, but Julian says there isn't enough room in the car.

We find some crackers on a table and feed them to Al on the way home. By the time we get home, just after ten o'clock, Allen has puked twice more (on the side of the road, thankfully) and passed out in the backseat of Julian's mom's car. We help him inside and find Mom, Dad, Keatie, and Paloma sitting around the living room table. Mom has been crying, and when she sees us at the door, she runs over to open it for us and help Allen in.

Allen wakes up. "Mom," he tells her, "I got sick."

"I know," she says. "I see." She looks at Haley. "You poor thing."

Haley smiles weakly.

"I'll take you home," Julian offers.

I look at Haley; she looks away. "I'm really, really sorry," I tell her.

"I know," she says. "We'll talk tomorrow."

Julian and Haley leave, and Mom and Dad take Al to his room to talk, leaving Keatie, Paloma, and me in the living room. Keatie gets out her violin and plays "Turkey in the Straw" for us over and over again.

"That's all I can do," she finally says. "My fingers hurt."

We sit in uncomfortable silence for a few minutes before I realize that Keatie has fallen asleep.

I nudge her gently. "C'mon, Keater, it's time for bed."

I help her to her room and into bed.

"Mia," she mumbles, half-asleep. "Is Allen bad now?"

"What?" I ask her, confused.

"Is he bad? Is he going to get kicked out of school and put in jail?"

"He's in trouble, Keatie, but I don't think he's going to jail. He isn't bad, he's just sad, I think."

"But we're all sad, right? Me and you and Mom and Dad. We all got sad."

"Yeah." I can barely speak. It's that simple, I guess. We all got sad.

"But don't worry, Mia. We can't be sad forever. It's no fun."

I sit with Keatie until she falls asleep. When I return to

the living room, Julian and Paloma are playing Uno. Julian and I go outside when the game is over.

"Some prom, huh," Julian says, putting his arms around my waist and pulling me to him.

"Yeah. Pretty memorable."

"Look, Meems, I'm sorry about what happened. I thought he'd sober up by the time we got to the dance."

"Hey, you were just trying to make everybody happy. It's not your fault."

"Yeah, but . . . I should've known. . . ."

"Let's not talk about it. Please."

I suddenly feel tired.

"I think not talking about things is what got everyone into this situation in the first place."

"Yeah. I guess so."

He kisses me. A good one. A real prom night kind of kiss. And then, too soon, it's over.

"I like you a lot," he says. "Thanks for being my date. Thank you for wearing that dress."

"Thank you for noticing," I tell him.

"I should've said something sooner. . . . I was so preoccupied with Al. . . ."

"Yeah." I yawn. "We all should have said something sooner."

Julian looks uncomfortable. "It's late. We should call it a night." He kisses me on the forehead, squeezes my hand. "I'll talk to you tomorrow."

"If I make it through the night."

"You'll be okay."

"Good night."

I say good night to Paloma and walk down the hall toward my room. When I pass Al's room, I expect to hear an argument in progress, but they are talking in soft voices. Without thinking, I open the door and walk in.

"Hi," I say. "I just wanted to say good night."

"Wait," Mom says.

"Can't I please just go to bed and try to forget this night?"

"In a minute," she says. She looks at me for a few seconds. "You're not wearing the dress we bought."

Dad looks confused.

"I'm wearing the dress I wanted to wear," I say.

"You look beautiful, Mia. Too grown-up, but beautiful."

"Thanks."

"But that doesn't mean it's okay to go sneaking around and ignoring my rules. There's been too much of that going on in this house."

Dad pipes up, "Paloma liked Mia's dress so much, she bought it in red."

"Yes, she did," I say.

"When did Paloma see your dress?" Mom asks.

"A story for another day," I tell her. "I'm going to bed."

"Okay. But we have a lot to discuss; tomorrow will be a big day," Mom says.

"I can hardly wait," I tell her.

"Night, Meezer," Allen groans from his bed.

"Night, Al."

changes

THE NEXT MORNING, WE HAVE A FAMILY COUNCIL, JUST LIKE some family on a cheesy TV show. Even Dad comes. Without Paloma. For a few minutes, I think Mom and Dad are going to tell us they aren't getting divorced anymore. They don't.

Instead, they tell us that we'll be going to therapy as a family for a while.

"We'd like you to help us out," Dad says. "We'd like to know what you think we can do to make it so that we don't have more nights like last night."

"I guess I need to learn to hold my alcohol," Allen says.

"Allen. This is not a joke," my dad warns him.

"Oh, actually, I think it is a joke. When the shit hits the fan, we're suddenly a family again? Is that how it works? This is new. When you guys decided to get a divorce, did you talk to us? Did we have a council about how to fix you two? So now that you've screwed us up, you want to fix things? Why didn't you try that before?"

"We did try it." My mom's voice cracks. "We decided the best way to fix things between us was to split up. I'm sorry that we left you out of that decision. We should have been more honest with you about what was going on, but we wanted to make things as easy as possible for you."

"Well, it hasn't been easy," he says, and he begins to cry. When Keatie sees this, she begins to sob; then my mom does; then I do. My dad looks on as if he wants to cry but can't find the tears.

Our family council ends in a loud, wet mess. But nobody is hurt, there is no vomit, there are no severed limbs. The fact that I am comforted by this is a little depressing. But at this point, I'll take what I can get.

the worst best friend

POST–FAMILY COUNCIL, I GO TO HALEY'S.

When she opens the door, I blurt out, "Mike Hickenlooper likes you and he wanted to take you to prom."

Haley doesn't look as surprised as I thought she would. "I know," she says.

"You do?"

"Come in, you dork."

We go to Haley's room, sit on her bed, and talk, kinda like we used to, only now things are a little weird between us.

"How did you know?" I ask her.

"Well, I didn't know for sure, but I figured when he started calling . . ."

"Oh . . . yeah."

"How did you know?"

"Julian told me."

"Why didn't you say anything?"

I play with a loose thread on her quilt, unsure of how to answer. I can't come up with anything but the truth. "Because I wanted you to go to the prom with Al, so that I could have my dream prom night and not have to worry about stuff."

Haley nods and is quiet for a while.

"I'm sorry," I tell her. "Really."

"Mia, the thing is, the prom isn't a big deal, really. I can go out with Mike whenever. It's just that . . ." She looks at me. Her eyes are red and watery. "I need you sometimes, Meems. You know? I need to talk. I need to be listened to. I know you think I'm this superhuman who doesn't have any problems, and maybe I don't have any that are as big as yours, but I still have some. And lately, you've just kind of vanished, you know? You disappeared."

"I didn't mean to," I tell her. "But I didn't know what else to do."

"Well, you can't just stop talking and try to hide everything."

"I know."

"This is going to sound stupid, I know, but you really hurt my feelings. Really."

At that moment, it feels like we are kids again, for some reason. Like we are just learning how to be friends. Somehow, while I was working so hard to protect myself and my feelings, I forgot about her feelings, and probably about everyone else's.

I think about my mom and dad and what my mom said about my dad's being a ghost, and I wonder if he was scared, too. If he forgot about everyone else and then just never remembered.

old habits

TEN DAYS LATER WE ARE IN LISZ'S OFFICE. ALL OF US: ME, MOM, Dad, Keatie, and Allen.

"So," Lisz starts, "I think the first thing we should do is discuss why each of you is here, what you hope to accomplish through attending therapy as a family."

No one says anything.

"Why don't we start with the parents? Maggie? Russ? Would one of you care to begin?"

They start to speak at the same time.

"Well, I think we should start with . . ."

"I'd like to know what's been going on . . ."

"Russ, I hardly think you should be the one to start, given the fact that you spend maybe an hour a week with the kids."

"This from the woman who didn't even know what her daughter was wearing to her prom?"

And so it begins. The healing process.

"Why don't I spend a few minutes with just the two of you first, before we bring the children into the discussion?" Lisz says.

"Great idea," says Allen, already out of his chair.

"I want to stay," Keatie says.

"See you guys later," I say, pushing Keatie toward the door.

We wait and wait, but Lisz does not call us back in. When the hour is over, my parents come out, looking as if nothing has changed between them.

"We'll definitely be meeting all together next week," Lisz tells us.

"I can't wait," I mutter.

"And you'll still have your regular Thursday appointments, too," she says, like she's telling me I just won fifty thousand dollars on *Jeopardy!*

And the weird thing is, I'm relieved when she says this. It means it's okay if I don't have everything figured out. It means I am not a ghost, a serial killer, a head-on collision.

About the Author

Olivia Birdsall grew up in Orange County, California, and Salt Lake City, Utah, and is the second of ten children. She lives in New York City, where she teaches writing at New York University and in public schools. Olivia spends her free time dreaming about exotic vacations, baked goods, and rock stardom. *Notes on a Near-Life Experience* is her first novel.